RIVAL REVENGE

Other books in the
CANTERWOOD CREST SERIES:

TAKE THE REINS

CHASING BLUE

BEHIND THE BIT

TRIPLE FAULT

BEST ENEMIES

LITTLE WHITE LIES

CANTERWOOD CREST

RIVAL REVENGE

JESSICA BURKHART

ALADDIN M!X

New York London Toronto Sydney

This book is a work of fiction. Any references to historical events, real people, or real locales are used fictitiously. Other names, characters, places, and incidents are the product of the author's imagination, and any resemblance to actual events or locales or persons, living or dead, is entirely coincidental.

ALADDIN M!X

Simon & Schuster Children's Publishing Division

1230 Avenue of the Americas, New York, NY 10020

First Aladdin M!X edition January 2010

Copyright © 2010 by Jessica Burkhart

All rights reserved, including the right of reproduction
in whole or in part in any form.

ALADDIN is a trademark of Simon & Schuster, Inc., and related logo
is a registered trademark of Simon & Schuster, Inc.

ALADDIN M!X and related logo are registered trademarks
of Simon & Schuster, Inc.

For information about special discounts for bulk purchases, please
contact Simon & Schuster Special Sales at 1-866-506-1949
or business@simonandschuster.com.

The Simon & Schuster Speakers Bureau can bring authors to your live event.
For more information or to book an event contact the Simon & Schuster Speakers
Bureau at 1-866-248-3049 or visit our website at www.simonspeakers.com.

Designed by Jessica Handelman

The text of this book was set in Venetian 301 BT.

Manufactured in the United States of America / 0816 OFF

10 9

Library of Congress Control Number 2009937529

ISBN 978-1-4169-9039-0

ISBN 978-1-4169-9874-7 (eBook)

To Ross Angelella, for coming up with "Versus"
(though the game's real name is waaay cooler)
and for having some of the best answers when we play at BF.
Best. Nights. Ever.
I feel like a cool kid when I hang out with you.

ACKNOWLEDGMENTS

Kate Angelella, editor of amazing, you have no idea how there's no way these books would be even half as sparkly without your influence, brilliance, and constant guidance. The only reason we're on book seven is because of what you've put into them. And the glittery stickers kind of help. . . . ☺ Thank you, thank you for working on these like you do and for supporting me every second from outline to copyedits and beyond.

Thanks so much to everyone at S&S, especially Jessica Handelman, Russell Gordon, Karin Paprocki, Mara Anastas, Fiona Simpson, Bethany Buck, Bess Braswell, Lucille Rettino, Venessa Williams, Nicole Russo, and Brenna Franzitta.

Monica Stevenson, the awesome models and assistants, thanks so much for making this cover so stunning.

Alyssa Henkin, just thinking about how this started . . . and where the series is now . . . thank you!

My awesome friends for backing Canterwood and supporting my writing—Ross Angelella, Mandy Morgan, Lauren Barnholdt, Liesa Abrams, and Aly Heller.

My reader girlies—you're the best! I heart you all and thank you for being on Team Canterwood!

Finally, Kate, saying you're my BFF doesn't really cover it—I think it's more like fan-girl territory. For real. ☺ I have the best times with you mocking really bad movies, dancing, and singing on the train. You've always got my back and it goes both ways. LYSMB!

RIVAL REVENGE

I

PLENTY TO PRACTICE

CHARM'S HOOVES POUNDED AGAINST THE indoor arena floor and helped drown out my own unwanted thoughts. He gathered himself, surged into the air, and bounded over the vertical with red-and-white-striped poles. We flew by the windows in the arena. Not even a hint of light came through—it was barely five thirty in the morning. I'd been at the stable since four forty-five.

My chestnut gelding and I were the only ones here. Monday morning lessons for the advanced team wouldn't start for another hour or so. My chest tightened at the thought. Callie and Eric would be here soon.

I urged Charm to keep up his canter. I didn't want to think about Callie, the best friend I'd lied to in order to protect her from the truth and had lost anyway. And I couldn't even begin to think about Eric, my amazing ex-boyfriend who had witnessed something so horrible it had ruined our relationship and any possible chance of us getting back together. I'd barely slept for the past two nights and I was edgy and exhausted—ever since my little white lies had all come crashing down around me at my birthday party on Friday night.

Charm and I had been practicing almost nonstop all weekend. It kept me busy and away from my other BFF and roommate Paige, who didn't believe my story about my initiating the kiss with Jacob. Paige wouldn't stop asking me about it, so I'd spent as little time in our room as possible all weekend. But on Canterwood Crest Academy's campus, there were few places to escape.

I looked up just as Heather Fox walked into the arena. Heather, the leader of the Trio, was my enemy most of the time, but she'd helped me out the night of the party. I slowed Charm to a trot, then a walk.

Heather's blond hair was pulled into a low ponytail and she had on black yoga pants and a casual T-shirt. She didn't have a lesson this morning, so why was she here?

I stopped Charm in front of her.

Heather folded her arms and started at me—her ice-blue eyes seemed to cut right through my thoughts.

"What?" I asked her.

"*What* is that I get hard-core practicing, but you're being insane. If Mr. Conner caught you jumping alone—you'd be in so much trouble."

"Coming from *you*?" I laughed, willing my voice to sound stronger than I felt. "You practice all of the time. You're here more than anyone. And it's not like I'm on the cross-country course—I'm in the stable."

Heather made an *Are you kidding me?* face. I silently agreed—my argument was weak.

Heather reached out and rubbed Charm's blaze. "I'm practicing because I *want* to. You're practicing because you're trying to ignore what happened on Friday."

"Heather, I have nothing to do *but* ride. Who cares why I'm doing it?"

She rolled her eyes. "Oh, puh-lease, Silver. Maybe you'd have more options if you stopped spinning the I-kissed-my-best-friend's-boyfriend lie. Why aren't you telling Callie the truth?"

"It *is* the truth," I lied. "I kissed Jacob. I cheated on Eric. Callie was crazy about Jacob and now she hates me. It is what it is."

Heather stared at me for a long second. Like Paige, she'd known I'd been lying that night.

"Don't make the mistake that I care, because I don't, but you need to tell the truth. Paige and I know you're lying. Tell Callie what really happened—whatever it is—because it's going to come out eventually."

But it couldn't. If Callie found out that Jacob had kissed me and had been trying to get me back since before summer vacation, she'd be devastated. I'd rather Callie lost our on-again-off-again friendship than her very first boyfriend who, when all was said and done, was a really amazing guy. Just a little . . . confused.

Charm shifted beneath me and I ran my hand down his neck. "Callie's happy. She may hate me, but she's got Jacob."

"Then at least tell the truth," Heather said. "The last thing I need to see is your mopey face every day."

"I'm *not* moping. Look, I just . . ." I shrugged, looking down at Charm instead of at Heather. "I want to be by myself for a while."

Heather raised her hands in an *I give up* gesture. "Fine. Be alone. Be miserable because you have no friends. But *don't* let it affect the team. I'm serious, Silver." She started to walk away, then turned back. Her gaze softened and her eyes weren't so piercing anymore. "Just don't make the mistake I did last year. Riding can't be everything."

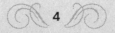

She walked out of the arena. I took a breath and looked out the door after her. I could leave right now and go get ready for class. Charm was probably tired after three days of nonstop practicing.

But instead, I turned him toward the arena's center and urged him into a trot. We had a few dressage moves to work on. There were plenty of other things to practice and I wouldn't be going back to my room until the last possible minute.

Heather had been wrong about one thing—riding *was* everything now. It had to be.

2

JUST CALL ME MARY

AN HOUR LATER, I OPENED THE DOOR TO MY
dorm room in Winchester Hall and started straight for
the bathroom to the shower.

I didn't want Paige to ask too many questions about
how long I'd been practicing. She knew I'd been out of the
room a lot and hadn't questioned me too much about it.
She'd known I'd had the most horrible Friday night of my
life and that Charm was like a security blanket for me.

"Are we going to the assembly together?" Paige asked.
She was still in her pink-and-white-striped pajamas. Her
red hair was wavy after she'd let it dry in loose braids last
night. She was looking over the outfit she'd chosen—a
black skirt, blue ballet flats, and an ivory scoop-neck shirt
with ruffles.

The assembly—ugh. I'd forgotten about that. I nodded and faked a smile. "Sure."

Inside the bathroom, I blew out a breath. I'd forgotten that classes for seventh and eighth graders would be
delayed this morning so we could attend an announcement from Headmistress Drake about Homecoming.
Apparently, Homecoming was a big Canterwood tradition
and even though it started next week, it was the *last* thing
I was interested in. I'd been so overwhelmed as the new
girl last year and being a part of an elite, scary-competitive
riding team, I'd somehow missed all of the festivities.

I showered, gathered my books, and headed to the
auditorium with Paige. My stomach flip-flopped at the
thought of seeing Callie, Jacob, or Eric. Callie would definitely ignore me and Jacob knew better than to even look
at me. He'd promised to never tell Callie that he'd confessed his feelings for me or that *he'd* been the one who'd
tried to kiss *me*. And Eric definitely wouldn't even look at
me. Confrontation wasn't his style. The way he'd walked
away on Friday night—he'd been so silent and furious, I
just knew it was the end.

I knew Eric well enough to know he was too upset
and angry to even think about taking me back. And I
was glad. It was better this way. I'd hurt him enough,

and beyond that, I'd messed up everything.

Again.

First with Jacob and then with Eric. I couldn't go through that again—trying to get him back only to have him say no. I needed time to get over Eric and the mess Jacob and I had created.

Paige and I walked into the auditorium, passed the ticket counter, and headed down a wide staircase with red carpet and glossy wooden handrails. If I hadn't been so upset about whom I might see, I would have enjoyed walking down the steps. I usually felt movie-star glam.

We took seats in the middle and I was glad for the darker lighting in the seats and the brighter light on stage. I fidgeted, worried about who would sit near me, but, to my relief, all of the surrounding seats filled with people I didn't know.

Then I saw them. Callie and Jacob walked down the aisle and took seats five rows in front of Paige and me. Callie's raven-colored hair was loose around her shoulders and she was in a black cotton dress with a three-quarters-sleeved pink cardigan I'd never seen before over it. Instinctively, I wanted to tell her that I liked it, but then I remembered I couldn't. She didn't look back. And neither did Jacob.

Eric walked by Paige and me and sat on the opposite side of the auditorium. Just looking at him made the room spin. I'd crushed him on Friday, letting him think I'd kissed Jacob. I looked down at my lap and my eyes stopped on my bracelet. I couldn't even think about how Eric felt after giving me a heart charm for my bracelet and then walking in on me with my hands on Jacob's chest. I'd been pushing Jacob away after he'd kissed me, but Eric hadn't realized that. He thought I'd always intended to go back to Jacob. I'd let him leave knowing there was no way I'd be able to convince him that it hadn't happened.

I stared straight ahead, focusing my attention on Headmistress Drake at the podium. Low, thick heels, a pencil skirt, and a brocade jacket ("Chanel," Paige whispered to me) made her look every bit what she was—headmistress of one of the most rigorous boarding schools on the East Coast.

"Welcome, seventh and eighth graders," she said. "Thank you for coming. I hope you're all excited to learn details about next week's Homecoming."

I folded my arms, just wanting this to be over. Beside me, Paige was leaning forward—hanging on the headmistress's every word.

"As you know, Homecoming week is one of Canterwood's most time-honored traditions," Headmistress

Drake continued. "We take great pride in our school and Homecoming is our chance to come together and celebrate Canterwood Crest Academy as the strong, elite institution that it is. We'll kick off Homecoming week with a football game on Monday night," she added. "I hope all of you will come to show support, not only for our team but also for our school. School spirit is important and cannot be underestimated."

Uh, nope. A football game was the last thing I'd be doing next week. No way. I had no desire to be surrounded by screaming fans, cheerleaders, or football players.

"While none of these activities are mandatory," Headmistress Drake said, "it is preferred that if your schedule allows for it, you should attend the pep rally before the game."

Homecoming = superlame and not at all where I wanted to be.

"We'll have festivities all week that will lead up to Friday when the king, queen, prince and princess of the junior royal court will be announced," Headmistress Drake continued. "Kings and queens are for the high school students, but there will be a prince and princess each from seventh and eighth grade."

Paige—and almost every other girl in the room—

practically started to hyperventilate. She reached over and grabbed my arm. I smiled at her—at least she'd enjoy it.

I tried to keep my eyes on Headmistress Drake, but I had to glance at Jacob. He was sitting on Callie's right, but I noticed his body was leaning slightly away from her. Jacob and I had theater class here way later in the day, but I didn't even want to think about that. What if he tried to talk me out of my decision? I knew I wasn't going to change my mind, but I wasn't even ready to hear him try to convince me to take him back.

I don't know how long I sat, zoned out, before I realized I'd missed the majority of Headmistress Drake's speech. I directed my attention back to her.

"Nominations for junior royal court will be made today," Headmistress Drake said. "Before you leave, you'll each grab two slips of paper. You'll write down one girl's and boy's name from your grade that you'd like to nominate for junior royal court."

At least that decision was a no-brainer. Paige and Ryan would be perfect. There was no one else I'd even consider nominating.

"Nominations will be posted in each dorm's common room on Sunday," Headmistress Drake said. "I wish you all the best of luck. Have fun with nominations. After

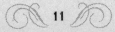

you've made your choices, please head to class. I hope you're all excited about Homecoming week. I look forward to cheering on Canterwood at the game!"

Rah-rah, I grumbled in my head.

Paige and I stood, bypassed a row of seats, and got in line for the nominations box. Everyone around us was chattering excitedly and girls were whispering in one another's ears about who they would nominate.

"What if every girl nominates herself?" I said. "Then what happens?"

Paige shook her head. "You could, I mean, no one can stop you, but there's going to be at least one honest girl who's going to vote for someone else. Or at least a few girls who are too scared that if they don't vote for their BFF, she'll do something awful to them."

I laughed. "So Julia and Alison won't be voting for themselves."

"Exactly." Paige smiled. "I'm nominating you 'cause you're my best friend."

We moved up a step in line.

"Paige," I said. "Do *not* do that!" I gently shoved her arm. "I don't want to be nominated! Plus, it's a wasted vote. Seriously. You're the only one who would nominate me. Pick one of your friends who actually has a chance at winning."

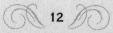

Paige stared at me for a second. "Okay. If that's *really* what you want."

"It is. Trust me. I'm nominating you and Ryan. You guys are perfect—I want you to win!"

Paige grinned. "Can you imagine? Ryan and me? I'd *die* if we won. I didn't care about Homecoming that much last year because I didn't have a possible date, but now . . ."

Ryan was Paige's crush. They'd gone out on a group date—that seemed so long ago—when Callie, Jacob, Eric, and I could actually be at the same table. Paige and Ryan had been flirty at my party on Friday. I knew it was only a matter of days before he asked her on a solo date. They were perfect together—Ryan was a sweet guy who genuinely liked Paige. And every time they were together, it eased Paige's shyness. Ryan was Paige's first almost-boyfriend and even though Paige gave the best guy advice, she was nervous around boys.

The line moved forward and Paige and I grabbed our slips of paper. We stopped at the banquet table and leaned over to write down our choices. On one paper I wrote *Ryan Shore* and on the other I wrote *Paige Parker.*

Easy.

Paige and I folded our slips of paper and dropped them into a big white box with a slit cut on the top.

SEVENTH AND EIGHTH GRADE NOMINATIONS was written on the side of the box.

"That was sooo cool," Paige said, grinning. "I love Homecoming already!"

I tried to muster up some fake enthusiasm. "Yeah," I said. "Awesome."

I wanted to ask Paige who she'd nominated, but I was too afraid of her answer. I was sure she'd say Callie. And I'd love it if Callie got nominated, but I just didn't want for Paige to even mention her name and start to ask more questions about Friday night. But Paige *did* have other friends. She might have picked Geena, one of her friends from cooking class.

Paige and I were quiet as we walked to Mr. Davidson's advanced English class. It was the coolest class we had—comfy chairs were arranged in a circle and the class was mostly discussion-based. It was a welcome break from the traditional classroom format.

"So," Paige said, pausing. She played with the gold circle on her necklace.

Paige and I had been instant BFFs from the second we met. We'd never fought about anything. But I knew she realized I was keeping something from her. And I knew it hurt her feelings. But I just couldn't. Not when

she was starting this relationship with Ryan. She was also Callie's friend. All I wanted was to pretend that night had never happened and to keep the rest of the semester drama-free.

Just then, Alison Robb, one third of the Trio, walked in and sat beside Paige. Alison and I had actually kind of become friends in a weird way. Not so much friends, I guess, but she was the one out of the Trio who I knew the best. Whenever Julia, the final part of the Trio, wasn't around, Alison was a pretty cool girl.

"Homecoming!" Alison said, grinning at us as she sat down.

And that's when I knew this was all I'd be hearing about until the end of next week.

"I know!" Paige said. "I'm *dying*. I can't wait."

I opened my notebook and tried to concentrate on reading my notes instead of listening to them.

"Omigod, the football game will be *awesome!*" Alison said.

Her voice was so high, it was impossible not to listen to her. Every sentence she and Paige exchanged ended with an exclamation point. Or two.

"Are you going with anyone?" Paige asked. "To the dance on Friday, I mean."

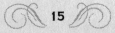

Alison shrugged. She tousled her sandy brown hair with one hand. "I don't think so. I don't know if anyone will ask me or not. Julia's going with Ben for sure. But I think Heather's going solo, so we'd just go together."

And I definitely wasn't going at all. Jacob and Callie would be there. Eric would probably go too, even if he didn't take a date. Plus, I had a bad track record with social events—like the Sweetheart Soirée and my birthday party—so I was staying far away from this one.

The other eight students straggled into the classroom and Mr. Davidson was right behind them.

"Welcome, class," he said. He pulled a well-worn copy of *The Secret Garden* from his pocket. "I hope you all had time to complete the reading and are ready to discuss the assigned chapters. Who wants to lead the talk?"

I raised my hand. Whenever I hadn't been riding Charm, I'd been studying. Getting good grades was right behind riding on my list of important things to do. I couldn't have even the tiniest thing get in my way of not staying on the Youth Equestrian National Team—the goal I'd worked so hard to achieve. If I lost the YENT . . .

"Sasha," Mr. Davidson said, pointing to me. "Go ahead."

"I . . . um . . . I related a lot to how Mary felt about

being in a new place," I said. "I felt that way when I first came to Canterwood. She didn't have any friends and when she meets Colin and Dickon, she finally starts to be happy. No one ever loved her and when she realizes she can love and that her friends love her back, she starts to enjoy her new home. But the place she feels most comfortable is the garden."

"And why do you think the garden makes her happy?" Mr. Davidson asked me.

"Because she can escape from everything and everyone. Maybe she can forget what's going on around her."

Mr. Davidson nodded. "Excellent. Thank you, Sasha." He looked around. "Who's next?"

Alison raised her hand. "I loved how Dickon was like an animal charmer. It was sort of like the snake charmers in India, where Mary used to live, and I wonder if that's why Mary liked him so much."

"Wonderful point, Alison," Mr. Davidson said. "Dickon felt familiar to Mary and her old life in India, so that's a great observation about her comfort with him."

I listened as the rest of the class discussed the book and how lonely Mary was until she had friends. The class debated about whether or not Mary would have wanted

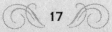

to run away from the mansion if she'd been the only kid and hadn't found Colin and Dickon.

I took a quiet breath. Even school was beginning to remind me of my current state of friendlessness.

3

TEMPORARY
QUARTET

I WENT STRAIGHT TO THE LUNCH LINE, NOT looking into the caf. All morning, I'd avoided thinking about lunch and where I'd sit. For a minute, I thought about hanging in the bathroom, but I couldn't. Then it would look as if I felt bad about what I'd done. And I couldn't give off that vibe. I had keep up my fake *Yeah I tried to steal a boy* act.

I never wanted Callie to question even for a second that I'd lied about what had happened with Jacob. Callie needed to hate me so she didn't look at Jacob and start to wonder about the truth. But, like Paige, Callie knew me well. Eventually, she'd start to think about Friday night and maybe she'd start to wonder about who to trust—her boyfriend or her ex-best friend.

I stepped forward in the line, still deep in thought. Paige would definitely want to eat with me, but I wanted more time on my own to think and not to have to answer any potential questions. I still worried that not eating with Paige would hurt her feelings.

"Hon?"

I looked up at the lunch lady, her hand hovering over the choices of salad dressing. "Yeah? Sorry?"

She smiled. "Ranch or Italian dressing?"

"Ranch, please."

I moved through the rest of the line and lifted my chin as I stepped into the cafeteria. I tried to channel Heather as I walked. She always looked confident and as if she didn't care what anyone thought. Maybe I needed to take secret lessons from her because that was exactly the feeling I needed to project right now.

Eric sat across from Rachel, her friends and Troy and Andy—Eric's friends. His back was to me.

I waited for jealousy to burn in my chest that Eric was sitting with Rachel, the pretty seventh grader who'd been openly crushing on him for a while. But nothing came. Not even one twinge of envy at seeing them together. I'd hurt Eric so much—he could sit with any girl he wanted—he deserved to have whatever he wanted.

Eric threw back his head, laughing. He must have felt the same—he didn't look as if he wanted to try and find me to talk anytime soon. He sat there smiling and laughing as if nothing bad had ever happened. As if *we'd* never happened.

That hit me.

Hard.

I choked down a sob and composed myself. I was on my own—the way I was supposed to be. I had to put my attention back on the things that mattered—school and riding. I was done with guys for a while.

At a table in the back of the caf, Jacob and Callie sat together. Jacob's eyes were on his plate as he picked through his curly fries. Callie's eyes flickered over, her dark brown eyes turning almost black when she glared back at me. I glanced away and hurried forward, almost tripping on a chair leg. I went to the back of the caf and let my tray clatter onto the table. The noisy chatter of the caf seemed unusually subdued today. For once, I actually wished for it to be louder so that I didn't have to hear my own swirling thoughts for one more second.

I sat down and saw Paige looking at me a few tables away. She motioned to me and mouthed *Come over.*

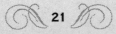

I half-smiled and shook my head. *I'm fine,* I mouthed back.

Paige stared at me for a second before turning back to her friends. She was sitting with Geena and a couple of girls from classes we didn't share.

My phone vibrated.

Ur prob not up 2 sitting w every1. Want me 2 come sit w u?

It was Paige.

No. Stay w ur friends. I'm gonna eat and run. But thanx. I texted back.

OK. But come over if u want.

Will do. <3

I speared a cherry tomato with my fork and started on my salad. I tried to focus on the tray in front of me, but my eyes kept glancing from Jacob and Callie to Eric and then to Paige. Paige seemed fine with her friends and like she'd accepted the fact that I wanted to eat alone. But I couldn't focus enough to eat. Being around all of them at once was harder than I thought.

"Silver."

Heather stared at me, one hand on her hip. She looked perfect—as always—in skinny black jeans, ankle boots, and a striking red V-neck T-shirt.

"What?"

"Get up and come sit with us. You're embarrassing yourself. I can't stop watching how ridiculous you look. Usually I'd just sit and laugh, but this is beyond pathetic."

I almost dropped my fork. "Sit with . . . you?"

Heather rolled her eyes. "Get your stuff now before I change my mind and decide to let you sit there and look like a total dork."

Even though she was insulting me, I didn't care. Sitting with the Trio was better than sitting with Paige—as awful as that sounded.

I grabbed my tray and hurried across the caf after Heather. Heads turned at every table as I shuffled by with Heather. Sasha Silver, the new outcast, walked with the most popular girl in eighth grade.

At their table, I sat beside Heather and across from Julia and Alison. Both girls raised their perfectly waxed eyebrows and stared at me. Julia couldn't have looked more disgusted to see me. She put down her spoon from her beef-and-veggie soup.

"What's going on?" Julia asked. She ran a hand over her chin-length blond bob, flicking strands angrily from her face. "Why is *she* sitting with us?"

"Because she looked ridiculous and it was annoying,"

Heather said. "I don't want Jas thinking she has even the smallest advantage over any of us. Silver's sitting over there looking like a kicked puppy."

I didn't even bother reacting to Heather's dig. At least I had someone to sit with. Even if it was the Trio. And even if everyone was looking at us.

"So we're pretending to like Sasha to . . . what?" Julia pressed.

Heather's blue eyes locked on Julia. I watched Julia shrink back a fraction. "Do I have to explain everything? We're making Jas insecure by acting like we're all together. She'll hate it."

Julia and Alison nodded.

But I knew that wasn't all this was about. Heather was being nice to me because she didn't want me to be alone. She'd never admit that to Julia, Alison, or me, though. Heather was the only person sitting at this table who had a feeling that I'd been lying about Friday, and for whatever reason, even though she really didn't like me, she seemed to respect what I'd done.

Alison smiled at me and took a bite of her Greek yogurt. But Julia just glared. We were all silent as we went back to our food. Julia obviously wasn't going to say anything in front of me that she wanted to keep among her friends.

"How's riding?" Alison asked, looking at Heather and me. She took a sip of her Diet Coke.

Heather gave her the *That's the lamest question ever* face. But I thought it was smart—it was a neutral topic and we could all talk about horses and riding, even though Julia and Alison weren't allowed to ride right now.

They'd been banned from riding until next January after they had been caught cheating on a history test. Alison had sworn to me that they were innocent, but I wasn't sure if they were or not.

"It's going pretty well for me," I said, deciding to jump in and answer the question. "I know I've got to do more dressage work with Charm so that we're ready for showing season."

The three girls nodded. I didn't want to say too much because I didn't want to make Julia and Alison sad that they couldn't ride. But Alison *had* asked about riding, so I didn't want to ignore her question and make it a bigger deal than it was.

"Aristocrat and I are doing great," Heather said with a half shrug. "All I care about is doing better than Jasmine. And we are." She took a bite of her ham-on-wheat sandwich.

"How are you guys doing?" I asked Julia and Alison.

Alison shook her head. "It's so hard. Every time I pass one of the pastures or arenas, all I can think about is how much I want to be in there riding. Especially since I didn't do anything to deserve being kicked off the team."

"That's the worst part," Julia said. "Whatever you think, Sasha, we didn't cheat. And we're stuck watching everyone else ride. But we're not just going to sit here and do nothing."

"You shouldn't," I said. "If you really didn't cheat, then you should prove it."

"We will," Alison said. "Trust me."

"Sooner or later, Jas'll make a mistake," Heather said. "We all know that she had something to do with it. She's more arrogant than ever since she made the YENT."

"And that's what's going to mess her up at shows, too," Alison said, shaking her head. "It's good for us that she thinks she's so amazing. She'll probably start to slack off soon, thinking she's got it, and then she'll be caught off guard with riding and what she did to us."

"I can't wait to watch it happen," Heather said.

And that was something we could all agree on.

"Change of subject, please," Alison said. "I don't want to even think about Jasmine King for another second."

"Agreed," Julia said, nodding.

Alison's eyes brightened. "Oooh, we have to talk about Homecoming!"

I looked at Heather and she didn't look thrilled about that topic. Maybe she wasn't into Homecoming either.

"Yeah!" Julia said. "It's going to be *amazing*. I can't wait for all of it—the football game, pep rally, dance, and everything."

I'd never seen Julia so excited about anything. What was it with everyone and this dumb tradition?

"Me too!" Alison said. She put her arms on the table, almost knocking over her glass of water. "I missed the football game last year. I'm going to paint my face and everything before I go."

"I don't think so," Heather said, shaking her head. "If you even open a tube of face paint, you're going to the game alone and you definitely won't be sitting with me."

Alison looked at the table for a second. "Yeah," she said after a few seconds. "I guess that would be kind of lame."

I'd always known it wasn't a democracy in the Trio, but I'd rarely witnessed Heather vetoing her friends' ideas.

"Are you just going to sit there, or what?" Julia asked, glaring at me. "Aren't you excited about Homecoming?"

I shrugged. "Not really. I've got a lot of stuff to do, so

I'm not going to the game or anything. Drake said nothing was mandatory."

Julia snorted. "Wow. Talk about school spirit, Sasha." Then she smirked. "But I can understand why you'd want to avoid the dance, at least. Your record with social events is pretty awful."

"Julia," Heather snapped. "Stop it. Silver is definitely already aware that she usually ruins dances or parties. Back off."

I almost didn't know what to do with that, but I knew better than to argue with Heather when she'd invited me over to their table. Plus, she'd defended me against Julia, even though it was wrapped with an insult.

"I think you'd have fun at the pep rally, though," Alison said. Her voice was extra cheery as if she was trying to ease the tension at our table.

"Maybe," I said. "I know Paige really wants me to go to all of the events, so I might consider going to something."

But I knew my mind was already made up—there was no way I was participating in *anything* Homecoming related.

4

LONGEST MONDAY EVER

BY THE TIME I GOT TO THEATER CLASS, I FELT like the only word that I'd heard all day was "Homecoming." It's all anyone wanted to talk about.

It was as if an army of people had put up flyers and banners about Homecoming the second after Headmistress Drake had made the announcement. Like people had been waiting and prepared with posters and had finally been given the okay to hang them. Hunter green and gold, the school's colors, dominated most of the REFUSE TO LOSE! and NOW FEAR THIS! posters that cheered on the school's football team. How could I have missed all of this last year?

At least the auditorium was poster-free, but I really just wanted to finish my class and get out. Throughout my history class with Jacob and Eric, I hadn't looked at either guy and they hadn't so much as glanced in my direction. It was what I wanted, but I hated the tension of the class.

This had to have been one of the longest Mondays ever. I'd sat through classes with Callie, Jacob, and Eric. Not exactly a great way to start the week. But all day I'd been making a list of everything I needed to do and the list kept growing. I needed to: work with Charm on everything from jumping to dressage, write a paper for history, devote more time to science class, and get ahead in all of my classes. And those were just the major things on the list.

I got up onstage to join the rest of the class, standing far away from Jacob. Our eyes met for a second and I glanced away. Jacob had promised to go along with my story and there was zero reason for us to talk. We both knew it was the only way we could prevent hurting Callie more than we already had. I didn't want it to get back to Callie that Jacob or I had so much as even glanced at each other.

"Hi, class," Ms. Scott, our teacher, said as she walked onto the stage. She wore her trademark red lipstick and her flatironed hair brushed her collarbone. She was just out of college and already one of my favorite teachers.

We all smiled back.

"We're going to warm up with a pairs theater game," Ms. Scott said. "Then, we'll get together and go over the homework and assigned reading."

Ms. Scott started naming the groups. "Sasha and Heather," she said, finally. "You're together."

I breathed a tiny sigh of relief. Heather was waaay better than Jacob.

Ms. Scott finished pairing us up then consulted her list. "Today's theater game is called 'park bench.' The rules are simple—one at a time, you're going to sit on the prop bench and pretend you're in a park. I'm going to give your partner a card that says who you—the person sitting on the park bench—are. The card will also tell your partner what role to play. Then, your partner is going to walk over, sit next to you, and react to seeing you. You have to give the audience enough so that we all can guess who you both are."

"Can we have an example?" a girl asked.

Ms. Scott nodded. "Sure. So, pretend you're sitting on the bench. My cue card says you're a high school basketball player and I'm a recruiter for a college basketball team. So, I'll go up to you and act like a recruiter. I'll start telling you about the awesome program at our school and

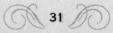

how you can't turn down my offer. You go along with it and hopefully you realize quickly who you are. Just don't come out and say who the person is. Keep it subtle and develop your characters."

That sounded easy enough.

"And you've got a minute to do this," Ms. Scott said.

Or maybe not . . .

She motioned for the first pair to step forward, gave a cue card to a girl, and the game started. A guy sat on the bench and the girl walked up to him.

"So, do you do all of your work in a coffee shop, like most people think you would, or do you work from your home?" the girl asked.

"It depends on how I'm feeling on that day," the guy said slowly. He had no idea who he was yet. "Sometimes, I just like to stay in and work."

"Do your fingers ever get sore from typing so much?" the girl asked. "Mine would. And how do you come up with your ideas?"

"So you and Jacob have decided not to even acknowledge each other's existence for an entire year?" Heather whispered to me. "I'm sure that will work out well."

I whispered back. "Why do you care?"

Heather laughed. "I *don't,* believe me. But we're on

the YENT. And I don't want us to ever look bad against Jasmine. I've said it a zillion times and I mean it."

"Waaait a sec," I said. "You keep flip-flopping. You just called me out yesterday for practicing too much. You told me to take it easy. And now you're worried that my personal life is a distraction and that it's going to mess up the team?"

Heather frowned. I'd actually won that argument. That *never* happened. Ev-er. Heather didn't know what to do about it.

"Oh, whatever. Forget it," Heather said. "But if you think you're gonna lose it—don't do it in the arena. Go cry in Charm's stall or something." Heather sighed and rolled her eyes. "Or talk to me if I have time, which I probably won't."

Our eyes met for a second. That was the biggest gesture of friendship Heather had ever made toward me. We still weren't friends, but we weren't exactly hating each other at this exact moment.

"Still. There's nothing to talk about," I said. "It's over. Jacob's with Callie. I'm completely focused on riding again, and that's how it's supposed to be."

Heather shot me a look and started to say something, but Ms. Scott walked over. "Heather and Sasha, your turn."

Oops. I'd completely missed all of the exercises before ours.

Ms. Scott handed me a folded card and motioned for Heather to sit on the bench. "Read the cue and start whenever you're ready," Ms. Scott said.

Heather walked over and sat on the bench while I opened the card.

Fan and movie star was written on the card.

I could do this—I'd seen enough episodes of *Inside Hollywood* where fans went crazy when they ran into stars on the street or in a coffee shop.

I stuck the card in my pocket and made my step bouncy as I walked over to Heather.

"Omigod, are you really her?" My voice was high and giggly.

"No," Heather said. "I get mistaken for Jordan all of the time."

"You're, like, lying," I said, sitting superclose to Heather on the bench. "You're totally her. You had that giant zit on your chin in a pic I saw in *Us Weekly* yesterday and it's still there."

Heather's gaze was frosty—no acting there. "It's makeup left over from a shoot. The makeup artist created that zit."

I bit my cheek so I didn't grin. Coming to class just for that moment was so worth it.

"Time," Ms. Scott said. "Class? Who are they?"

A girl in the second row raised her hand. "Sasha's a fan girl and Heather's an actress."

I nodded. "Yep."

"Good job, girls," Ms. Scott said. "Please take your seats. The next pair can come on up."

And for the next half hour, I watched the rest of the pairs act out whatever was on their cue card. Everyone did a great job and someone in the class was always able to tell who the actors were portraying. It was a fun game for everyone and I liked it more with each pair that I watched.

"Thanks, everyone," Ms. Scott said. "I'll see you next class. Read the assigned chapters and keep practicing the memorization techniques we've worked on. Please put your homework on my desk before you go."

It was my goal to be the first one out of there. I grabbed my backpack and Heather was beside me, creating a one-girl barrier between Jacob and me. Jacob was getting his stuff ready to go too, but I didn't look at him as I shoved my books into my backpack.

At least I had a real reason to hurry. Today, my YENT lesson was next. That was the cool thing about

theater—the elective was held at different times during the week. I was especially glad to go from theater—a class I had to share with Jacob—to riding. Plus, at this time of the day, Callie and Eric wouldn't be at the stable.

I put my paper on Ms. Scott's desk—it was a definite A. It was a page longer than required and I'd even asked if there was something I could do for extra credit. My grade in the class was already an A, but I wanted to keep it up as high as I could.

Heather put her paper on top of mine and together, we walked out of the auditorium and toward the stable. Heather looked at me and sighed. "You're not going to be weird for the entire lesson, right?"

"Nope," I said. "I swear—I'm fine. You'll see in the arena. I'm over last weekend."

Except for losing Callie, I wanted to add. *And Eric. And Jacob.*

As we walked, people stared after us. It had to be the last thing anyone expected to see—Heather and me walking together. Everyone had probably thought sitting at their table once for lunch would be the end of it and we'd go back to fighting like we always had. Even *I* thought it would be that way. Apparently, I was wrong.

Heather and I slipped into stalls in the newly reno-vated bathroom and changed into our riding clothes. The once-tiny bathroom now had three separate stalls, a wider mirror, two sinks, and way more counter space.

We got our horses' tack and split up in the aisle. Heather went to Aristocrat's stall and I went to get Charm. I gathered his lead line in one hand and opened the stall door. Charm whirled around, ears flicking back and forth anxiously.

"Oh, I'm sorry," I said. I always said hi to Charm before I went in his stall. I rubbed his neck, then snapped the lead line to the ring on his halter. He stood still while I clipped him into crossties and picked his hooves. Charm leaned into me as I brushed his shoulder. I ignored him and kept grooming him. I switched to the dandy brush and flicked dirt from his legs. Charm, turning his head as much the crossties allowed, tried to nudge my arm.

"What?" I asked, then realized my tone was sharper than I'd intended.

Charm blinked at me. "Oh, boy, I'm sorry," I said. I let the brush fall into his grooming box and hugged him. "It's not you. It's . . . everyone else. You're always on my side and I was mean to you. I need to remember that I'm not alone in the arena when I've got you."

Charm nodded and rubbed his cheek against my upper arm.

"We're going to get it back, Charm. We'll be awesome—like we were before I got all mixed up with Jacob. And Eric. And then Jacob *and* Eric." I sighed, pausing to think for a second. "I don't think I ever completely lost focus on riding. I just . . . got so caught up in drama. I'm sick of it—seriously. Done. Over it."

And I was. I'd panicked for what felt like *years* to try and keep Callie and Jacob together after his confession that he still liked me. But it hadn't mattered. Everything had shattered around me. I couldn't take another week of crazy-intense drama.

I finished grooming Charm and tacked him up. He lowered his head, making it easy for me to bridle him, and I slid the reins over his neck. I put on my helmet and walked him to the indoor arena. Heather and Jasmine were inside, both girls just mounting their horses and starting their warm-ups.

I stopped for a second—saddened by the first thought that popped into my brain: Callie wasn't in my class—*and I was glad.*

When I'd first started YENT lessons without her, I'd been devastated. She was on the advanced team and I was

on the YENT and I'd felt alone without one friend in the arena. We both hated not being able to ride together every day. But now, I was glad. If Callie and I had to practice together every day it would be beyond uncomfortable. Practices weren't going to be about boys or best friends— they were going to be about riding. And I was going to make up for my ridiculous last couple of lessons by wowing Mr. Conner from now on.

I mounted Charm and guided him to the wall. He settled behind Phoenix, Jasmine's gray gelding. Ahead of us, Heather and her darker chestnut, Aristocrat, trotted forward at an even pace. Aristocrat was a top-notch horse, but Heather also knew how to bring out the best in him. Heather's black boots gleamed, her fawn-colored breeches were spotless and, like always, her white polo shirt was horse hair free. It was still a mystery to me how she managed that.

I let Charm walk for a couple of strides before easing him into a trot. His movements were smooth and he followed behind Phoenix, but didn't tailgate. We made several laps around the arena, every one of us focused on her horse. Jasmine's gaze, intense as always, was narrowed between Phoenix's ears. She kept a tight grip on the reins and didn't give him any room to move freely.

Mr. Conner walked inside and stopped in the arena's center. He had a thick notebook in one hand and a Canterwood Crest travel mug in the other. Steam rose from the top and he took a sip.

"Hi, girls," Mr. Conner said. "Before we get started, I want to let you know that next week I will be taping a lesson to share with Mr. Nicholson."

Mr. Nicholson was the YENT's head scout—he'd chosen all of us for the team.

"It will be a regular class and there's no reason to think you need to schedule extra practice sessions or to worry," Mr. Conner continued. "You're all doing fantastic and I'm sure Mr. Nicholson will agree."

But my brain was barely able to process the last sentence. Jasmine and Heather were doing fantastic—Charm and I weren't! We needed to work harder before Mr. Conner filmed the lesson. Otherwise I'd look ridiculous next to my teammates. I'd have to make room in my schedule to ride more. I started making a mental list of things I could cut out of my schedule.

"I don't want the camera to throw off anyone during the taping, so I'm going to start bringing it to classes," Mr. Conner said. "I'll set it up but leave it off so that you and your horses get used to seeing it."

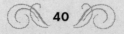

We all nodded.

"Let's get started, then," Mr. Conner said. "I want to work on flying lead changes today. You were all asked to perform them during your test for the advanced team, but we haven't practiced them for quite a while."

My stomach dropped. Charm and I could do flying lead changes—most of the time. But it had been *forever* since we'd done them.

"Flying lead changes are a natural movement for horses," Mr. Conner said. "But sometimes, a horse gets lazy and forgets how to pay attention to signals for a flying lead change."

Jasmine covered a yawn as if this conversation bored her.

"We're going to work the horses at a canter for a couple of minutes to be sure they're fully warmed-up and then you'll each take turns doing the exercise," Mr. Conner said. "Go ahead to the wall and start cantering."

We each moved our horses to the wall and Charm went quickly from a trot into an even canter. I moved with him and didn't bounce in the saddle—Charm's canter was too smooth for that. As we finished the warm-up, I contemplated how many more hours of riding I could squeeze into this week. I'd keep adding things to the list of activities that I could cut out. I'd see less of Paige, but she'd

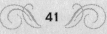

understand that I'd want to practice harder for the tape.

"Okay, slow to a walk, then line up your horses over there," Mr. Conner said, pointing to the far side of the arena. Jas, Heather, and I moved the horses to the arena's side and waited for Mr. Conner's instructions.

"Jasmine, you're going to go first," Mr. Conner said, uncapping his pen and holding it over his paper, ready to take notes on her performance. "Do you need a reminder about how to ask for a flying lead change? Or are you comfortable without instructions?"

I looked over at Jas—she held back a smirk. "I've got it, Mr. Conner," she said.

No surprises there.

He waved his hand at her. "Whenever you're ready."

Jas leaned down to adjust her left stirrup, then righted herself in the saddle. She sat straight, without being rigid, and her hands were soft on the reins. She asked Phoenix for a canter and the gray gelding responded immediately. They swept past Heather and me for two laps before Jas turned Phoenix toward the center of the arena. When she and Phoenix reached the center of the arena, I didn't even see Jasmine ask for the flying lead change—it just happened. Phoenix swished his tail and struck out with his opposite foreleg, then leading with that leg. Jas cantered

him back to us, grinning. There was nothing Mr. Conner could say about that. It was perfect.

"Beautiful, Jasmine," Mr. Conner said. "Your cues were subtle. Phoenix knew exactly what you wanted."

Beside me, Heather groaned under her breath. "What. Ever," she whispered. "We can do better."

I gulped. *She* probably could. But I wasn't so sure if *I* could. Sometimes, Charm ignored my cues. *Stop it,* I told myself. I was freaking myself out before I even started. And I didn't want Charm to feel any tension from me.

"Go ahead, Heather," Mr. Conner said. Jas angled Phoenix next to me and we watched Aristocrat and Heather mimic what Jas and Phoenix had just completed. Like Jas, Heather's signals were invisible. Aristocrat's flying lead change made him look as if he belonged at a junior class in the Hampton Classic. His movements were gorgeous.

Heather circled him for another half lap before slowing him and riding back over to Jas and me.

"Wonderful, Heather," Mr. Conner said. "Your hands were perfect. That was exactly the way to ask for a flying change."

There was no way Charm and I could do as well as Jas and Heather—it was a fact—but we could try.

Mr. Conner marked something on his paper, then turned to me. "Ready, Sasha?"

I nodded. "Yes."

Charm seemed to know I needed encouragement—he walked forward before I could think about what we were about to do. I let him trot and posted as he moved away from Phoenix and Aristocrat. I squeezed my legs against his sides and urged him into a canter. We circled the arena twice and then I pointed him to the center.

Relax, I told myself. In four strides, I'd ask Charm for the change. I only had seconds before it was time. I switched my leg positions, moving my opposite leg behind the girth, and kept my hands light. Charm stretched through his back and for a second, I wasn't sure he was going to do it. But I felt him shift and he switched lead legs.

Score! We'd done it! I hid my smile and patted his neck when we reached the other side of the arena. "Nice job, boy," I said.

"Sasha, good work," Mr. Conner said, smiling at me. "Charm hesitated for a second as if he wasn't going to follow through, but he listened to your cues."

"Thanks," I said.

"Let's keep up the flatwork practice," Mr. Conner said.

"Reverse directions and start trotting, please."

Charm and I were focused and sharp. I kept all of my attention on him, making sure he listened every second. I kept pressure on him with my hands and legs.

"Sasha, ease up a little," Mr. Conner called. "You can give Charm space—he's been attentive the entire class."

I nodded and relaxed my grip on the reins, letting Charm lower his head a fraction. He snorted and dipped his head down.

"Let's work on flexibility," Mr. Conner said. "I'm going to set up a few poles at the end of the arena and you'll canter through those. While I set them up, please trot your horses and keep them warmed-up."

Mr. Conner set up four white poles with weighted bases. He nodded to Jasmine. "You may go first. When you reach the last pole, turn Phoenix around and do the exercise in reverse."

Jasmine pushed down her heels. "Okay."

She cantered Phoenix to the end of the aisle, bypassing the poles and then slowing him to a trot before halting him in front of the first one.

She waited for a second before heeling him forward. He accelerated into a smooth canter and his gray mane whipped from side to side as he moved through the poles.

Jas bent with him, moving easily from side to side in the saddle. She turned him sharply at the final pole and his hooves kicked up arena dirt as they curved around the pole and started the exercise again. Jasmine weaved him through the final pole, then let him into a wide half circle to start back to us.

"That was great, Jasmine," Mr. Conner said. "Phoenix is an agile horse and I think he'd benefit even more from exercises such as these."

And so would Charm and I.

"Sasha, you may go ahead," Mr. Conner said.

I trotted Charm to the first pole and turned him to face it. I sat deep in the saddle, gripping with my knees and preparing for the weaving movement through the poles. I tapped my heels against Charm's sides and urged him into a trot for a few strides before giving him rein to canter.

We cantered straight for the first pole as if we'd ram into it, then at the last second I pulled him to the side. Charm shifted from side to side and weaved through the poles as if we did it every day. I shifted to the side each time he moved and I didn't lose my balance for a second. Before the last pole, I sat deep in the saddle, slowing Charm a fraction to round the last pole in the first

run-through. He leaned so far sideways, I thought we'd tip over, but I'd seen enough pole bending to know how far horses could lean over without tipping. And Charm and I weren't even close to that.

We went through the rest of the poles and I trotted Charm back to join Heather and Jasmine. I patted his neck and he arched it under my touch. He knew we'd killed it.

Mr. Conner's smile said it all. "Beautiful, Sasha. I can tell that you've been working on flexibility exercises for yourself and they show. Nice work."

Heather rode next and her ride was flawless. Aristocrat tossed his head as he joined us. He and Charm eyed each other—both horses raising their heads. White showed in the corner of Aristocrat's eyes and he tugged the reins through Heather's fingers. He and Charm hadn't gotten along since the first day Charm and I had arrived on campus.

"Nice work, everyone," Mr. Conner said. He closed his notebook and smiled at us. "You all continue to impress me with your work ethics. Again, please remember to take extra time cooling your horses even though we were indoors because of the heat. See you tomorrow."

Jas, Heather, and I dismounted. I eased the reins over Charm's head, then loosened his girth. His chest was

warm and there was sweat around his saddle pad, but he wasn't too hot. I started walking him in circles around the arena. All I could think about was what time I was going to get to the stable tomorrow morning to practice.

5

AT AN IMPASSE

I DRAGGED MYSELF THROUGH MY DOOR almost an hour and a half later, exhausted. Paige looked up at me from her spot in front of her closet. She was adjusting her blue wrap dress and there was a pair of silver kitten-heels by her purse.

"Where're you going?" I asked. I plopped onto the floor and pulled off my riding boots, setting them on our shoe carpet.

Paige smiled. "Ryan texted me while you were out and asked if I wanted to grab a slice of pizza."

"That's *great!*" I said. "I know you'll have so much fun. If not, SOS text me and I'll call you with some emergency. Like I ran out of lip gloss and we have to go get some ASAP."

"You better!" Paige said. "But I think you're right—we will have fun."

Paige sat at her desk chair and unzipped her makeup case.

"Ooh, allow me," I said. "I'll do your makeup."

Paige glanced down at the bag, then back at me. "I'd love that. But you have to do something first."

"What?"

Paige turned her full gaze on me. "You have to tell me what really happ—"

"No," I interrupted. "There's nothing to tell, Paige. Why do you keep asking? Everything went down exactly like I told you. If you're trying to spin it so that I'm innocent and you don't have to be mad at me for trying to steal Jacob—don't. I'd understand if you thought what I did was horrible."

Paige sighed. "I'm your best friend. Do you really think I can't tell when you're lying?"

It was my turn to sigh. "I'm *not* lying. And you're *my* best friend too. So you should believe me."

Paige blinked a couple of times. "I know you. You'd never go after a girl's boyfriend—especially if he was with your best friend." Paige played with her eyelash curler. "I wish you trusted me enough to let me help. Something's obviously going on and you're lying about it. No matter what it is, Sash, you know you can trust me."

I moved over and sat at the end of my bed so I was closer to Paige. "I *do* trust you. You're my best friend and if I need help, you're always the first one I go to. I promise—things are fine. I know you think something's going on, but it's only making things worse when you keep bringing it up." I looked at my hands for a second. "I'm trying to forget about Friday and when you keep bringing it up, it doesn't help."

Paige and I stared at each other for a few seconds, then she reached for her eyeliner and turned her attention to the mirror. I grabbed *The Secret Garden* from my nightstand. Paige and I didn't say another word to each other as she applied a final coat of lip gloss, smoothed her dress, and put on her shoes. Her hand was on the doorknob when she turned back to me.

"I'll never stop being your friend. You can try to make yourself look like the bad guy, but I know better. Something else happened."

Paige opened the door and it closed behind her as she disappeared into the hallway.

I rubbed my eyes with my fingers and when I lowered my hand, my charm bracelet caught the light and glittered

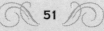

in front of me. I touched each charm. The horse from my parents and the horseshoe and heart from Eric.

I stared at them for a long time. I knew what I had to do, but it was hard.

I held up my wrist and unfastened the charms from Eric. I looked at my bracelet—lonely with only one charm. I got up, walked over to my desk and pulled open a drawer. I found a tiny jewelry box and put the charms inside. I closed the drawer on the heart and horseshoe.

And, finally, on my relationship with Eric.

6

TOTALLY MY
LUCK

WHEN I WALKED INTO HEALTH CLASS ON
Tuesday, Ms. Utz was clearly excited about something.
She was bustling from one end of the classroom to the
other—her large frame almost bumping into desks in the
front row.

I sat down next to Paige.

"Did she drink a gallon of coffee, or what?" Paige
whispered.

"Don't know," I said. "I've never seen her move so fast."

My eyes flickered to the doorway and I watched Jacob
walk into the classroom. He sat on my other side and neither of us looked at the other.

I shuffled through my health notebook, pretending to
be busy as Ms. Utz took attendance.

After she finished, she turned to us with a scary grin. "As a class, you're about to start a new project with a partner. You both will spend a week taking care of an egg. You'll log where you take your egg, document it with photos, and you and your partner must work out custody of the egg."

An *egg*?! Seriously? That was sooo not in the syllabus, and Utz had never mentioned it when she'd talked about what we'd be doing during the class. Plus, this sounded like the worst project *ever*. I didn't have time to care about a dumb egg when I had a zillion other things to do!

"Let me announce the partners and then I'll go into specifics," Ms. Utz said. She started naming the pairs. Paige got Aaron, a guy who was in our English class. He was as crazy about grades as Paige, and I knew they'd be good partners.

"Sasha," Ms. Utz said. "You'll be working with Jacob."

I didn't even react. Of course Jacob and I were working together. It was totally my luck. Callie was going to think I'd planned this or something.

Ms. Utz handed each team an egg. She gave ours to me along with a small spiral notebook. "You must arrange times to trade off babysitting your egg," she said. "You cannot leave it in your room all day while you attend sports or class. Someone must always be watching it. The more photos you take of your egg with you in different places, the better your grade."

So Jacob and I were going to have to meet up a lot for a week. *Greeeat.*

"Before you leave class," Ms. Utz said, "decide who's going to take your egg and when you're going to trade back. If it breaks, come see me."

How was Utz going to know if we were watching the egg or not? I thought to myself.

"Before we start reading chapter three, does anyone know the purpose of the egg exercise?" Ms. Utz asked.

To torture us, I thought.

A girl in the front row raised her hand. "It is to teach us how to work together and be responsible for something?"

Ms. Utz nodded. "Yes, Krista, exactly. The goal is for you and your partner to take care of this egg and to get a feeling for what it's like to be responsible for something. Even though the egg is obviously inanimate, it will provide a great start for you and your partner to learn to be accountable for something fragile—like a child or a pet."

I laid the egg on top of my sweater that was sticking out of my backpack. This was so ridiculous. What if we already had a pet? Charm was waaay more responsibility than an egg.

I looked over at Paige and she shot me a sympathetic look. *Sorry,* she mouthed.

I shrugged.

"Jacob, you may start with the chapter," Ms. Utz said.

Jacob looked down at his book. "Healthy eating is as important for the body as exercise," he read. And as he talked, I closed my eyes, listening to the sound of his voice. I'd missed hearing him speak.

I opened my eyes and made myself listen to him talk about the food pyramid, which we'd all learned about in, like, second grade. I almost wished he was reading about something I'd never heard about before so I'd have to concentrate on the words and take notes instead of listening to his voice.

I couldn't do *that*—waver. I'd made my choice and I couldn't go back and forth. Because if I started to think about Jacob, then my mind wandered to Eric. And I missed him so much even though I refused to think about it.

After we finished going through the chapter and Utz assigned homework, she dismissed the class.

"I have to go to riding," I said to Jacob. I looked at my bag while I talked to him. "Do you want to take it first?"

Jacob gathered his stuff and stood. "Sure. And we can text or something tomorrow and trade."

I handed the egg to him, careful that our fingers didn't touch. "Here's the notebook," I said.

Paige was still busy trading info with Aaron, so I waved at her and walked out of the classroom. She'd understand that I didn't want to stay in here with Jacob.

Later that afternoon, I went to my riding lesson. I walked into the tack room and Julia and Alison were inside.

"Hey," I said. I put Charm's saddle pad over my arm and reached to grab his saddle. I noticed that his tack was filthy—how embarrassing. I needed to clean it ASAP.

"This isn't going to last much longer," Julia said.

"What?" I asked.

Julia rolled her eyes. "Alison and I not riding. We're going to be back in the saddle sooner than anyone thinks."

Alison glanced at Julia, then at me. "We can't keep watching everyone else ride. It's killing us."

I put Charm's saddle over my arm and grabbed his

bridle. "I'm sorry it's so hard. Maybe you guys should avoid the arenas when lessons are going on. Take Trix and Sunstruck for a walk on the trails. You know they want to get out too."

Alison nodded. "That's a good idea. We've got to do something. They're going crazy in their stalls, even though Mike rides them whenever he has time."

"But Mike's not you guys," I said. "I get it."

I left them in the tack room and groomed and tacked up Charm. I couldn't imagine being in Julia's and Alison's position. I'd die without Charm and he'd never be happy with a stranger riding him. It had to torture Alison and Julia every time they stepped into the stable. Their ban from riding wasn't lifted until January and they had a looong way to go till then.

I put on my helmet and led Charm to the indoor arena. I mounted and started warming him up. I leaned down and hugged his neck, grateful to have him.

"How sad," Jas said, entering the arena on Phoenix. "You don't have a boyfriend so you've resorted to making out with your horse."

"That's exactly what I was doing," I said. "You caught me."

I looked away and trotted Charm forward. I was

actually glad when Heather rode inside. At least Jas
would keep her mouth shut—sort of—when Heather
was around. We all warmed up our horses while waiting
for Mr. Conner.

I halted Charm, backed him up, and then started him
at a trot. A few strides later, I slowed him again and began
working him in circles that got smaller and smaller.

"I know you're dense, but practice hasn't started yet,"
Heather said. "This is called a *warm-up*." She said the last
two words slowly.

"We are," I said. "Whatever."

Before I could turn Charm in the opposite direction,
Mr. Conner entered the arena with a smile. We halted our
horses in front of him.

"Hi, girls," Mr. Conner said. "I'd intended for us to
practice inside today, but Ms. Walker asked if we could
swap arenas so the advanced team could work inside. We
hired her just to work with the beginner and intermediate
teams, but when my schedule is full, she's going to take
over the advanced team. So, let's move to the largest outdoor arena and we'll get started."

Mr. Conner walked toward the door and we turned
our horses toward the exit, then dismounted. I led Charm
toward the door and just as Heather, Jasmine, and I

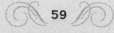

reached the wide doorway, Callie, Eric, and the rest of the advanced team started into the arena.

I almost stopped walking when I looked up at Callie and Eric. They were riding side by side and laughing. I pulled Charm forward, jogging to get away from them. I didn't want to watch them together. Eric wouldn't trash-talk me to Callie or anyone—he wasn't that kind of guy. But it made me feel weird to see them together. And I couldn't think about that before a lesson. Especially not when we were getting closer and closer to the tape for Mr. Nicholson.

By the time we got settled in the outdoor arena, I was ready for a tough lesson. I wanted Mr. Conner to push us hard so we'd be ready for the tape.

"Let's start with a sitting trot," Mr. Conner said.

Jasmine, Heather, and I trotted the horses around the arena and I pushed my tailbone into the saddle.

"Canter," he called.

At the same second, Charm, Aristocrat, and Phoenix leaped into canters and they made their way around the arena.

"Walk," Mr. Conner said.

We slowed the horses and I waited for Mr. Conner to tell us what to do next. I hoped for dressage—Charm and I needed more work.

"Trot for two laps and then change directions," Mr. Conner said.

I tried not to roll my eyes. This lesson was so basic! Where was the trot-without-stirrups-until-you-die Mr. Conner? This wasn't even close to the work we needed.

When he told us to cool out our horses, I almost wanted to raise my hand and ask if that was *really* it.

"See you next class," Mr. Conner said.

I half-expected him to turn around and say he was kidding and there was no way we were getting off that easy. But he left the arena and didn't come back.

I dismounted and pretended to be cooling Charm. I walked him around the arena until Jasmine and Heather left. Before going inside, I peeked through the indoor arena to make sure the advanced class was gone. The space was empty so I led him inside, mounted, and urged him into a trot. We had lots more work to do—there was no way that lesson was enough.

I sat deep in the saddle, pushing my heels down and keeping my hands still. We made figure eights through the center of the arena and I took advantage of having the entire space to myself. I kept one eye on the door, though. If Mr. Conner saw us practicing after already having a lesson, he'd make us stop. But I remembered

that he had a grain and hay shipment arriving today, so I hoped he was busy.

Besides, you couldn't even call what we'd just done a "lesson." It was more like a warm-up.

After figure eights, I stopped Charm and worked on my own posture. I dropped the reins around his neck and stretched my hands to the ceiling. I spent half an hour going through balance and strengthening exercises so Charm could rest. I twisted in the saddle and an incoming horse and rider made me stop in mid-twist.

Callie and Black Jack. Callie halted Jack, mounted, and then looked at me. Her glare made me shrink a little into my saddle. I was used to that look from Jasmine and Heather—not Callie.

"You just finished a lesson, right?" Callie asked, her tone clipped.

"Yeah."

"Then, do you mind?" But the way Callie said it—she wasn't asking a question.

Charm shifted under me, feeling my nerves. "Of course you can ride in here too," I said. "I don't care."

I had to hold myself back from telling her that I *wanted* her in here with me, that I had to tell her what really happened, and that I missed her. But I didn't.

Callie laughed, but there was no humor behind it. "No. I meant, do you mind *leaving*? I want to practice inside. Alone."

I paused. "Uh, sure. But you finished your lesson when I did, so—"

"So what? I want to practice more." Callie stared at me from under her helmet. "It's the least you can do, don't you think? I mean, after what you did."

Her comment made me freeze. I didn't know what to even say. But I knew I had to keep up the facade that I didn't care about our friendship. She had to keep believing that I thought going after Jacob had been worth it.

"Callie, I—" I stopped when Heather walked into the arena. She led Aristocrat over and looked up at us. Of course she'd had the same idea to practice more—we all had. She'd probably gone to grab a soda or something.

"Are you *really* trying to kick her out, Callie?" Heather asked. She folded her arms. "That's not happening. We're riding in here too, so practice with us or go somewhere else."

Callie's head jerked back a little. This felt surreal. It was suddenly Heather and me versus Callie.

"Wow, a turf war." Jasmine, without Phoenix, walked into the arena and grinned at all of us.

"You're not riding at all, so you have no reason to

be in here," Heather said to Jas. "Get out."

Jas put a hand on her hip, her eyes flashing at Heather. "Whatever, Heather. Like I'm going to let you and Sasha force Callie out. I mean, I don't like any of you, but Sasha . . ." Jas shook her head. "This is just wrong. You went after your BFF's boyfriend. All she did was ask you to leave the arena so she could practice and you run and get Heather to stand up for you?"

"I didn't get Heather to do anything," I said, trying to keep my voice quiet. If I yelled, Mr. Conner would be in here in two seconds. "I was here first, then Callie showed up. I'm not leaving."

"You're ridiculous," Jas said. "You should have *offered* to leave. Everyone at school knows what you did. You're the girl who tried to steal a boyfriend from her best friend. You really should just resign from the YENT and go home. No one wants you here."

I blinked back tears. I'd tried not to think about what anyone else had thought about me and my reputation on campus. And I wished I could believe that Jas was exaggerating, but I wasn't sure. Did everyone think that?

"Jasmine, shut up," Heather said. "You have no idea. So don't pretend to know anything about what's going on around campus."

Jas's face went pink. This had to stop. I wanted to practice, not fight.

"I'm staying on campus *and* in the arena," I said. "So deal."

Jas shrugged. "Fine. Stay and let everyone talk about you. More fun for me." She turned and walked out of the arena.

Without a word, Heather mounted Aristocrat and trotted him to the far end of the arena and started riding him in large circles. I edged Charm toward the middle and went back to working on my stretches. Callie, as if deciding what to do, looked at the door, then turned Jack to the empty corner of the arena and began working on transitions.

I sneaked a glance at Callie. She looked focused and not at all as if she was thinking about what had just happened. Before the Jacob mess, if Jas had ever said anything like that to me, it would have been Callie defending me—not Heather.

It used to be Callie and me against the Trio. Now, Callie was looking at me as if I was on the opposite side.

7

OUT OF ALL
THE ROOMS

I STAYED IN THE ARENA UNTIL I FELT CHARM'S
stride start to lag. I took extra good care of him—giving him
two carrots and grooming him until he was super shiny.

"You were perfect today," I told him. I hugged him and
he wandered right to his hay net. I latched his door, put
away his grooming box, and picked up his tack.

I took his saddle and bridle into the tack room, filled a
bucket with warm water, and got out a tin of saddle soap.
I undid every buckle on his bridle and saddle, embarrassed
that I'd let Charm's tack get so dirty. I scrubbed with
the yellow soap until it caked under my fingernails and
water ran down my elbows. My fingers got tired as I ran
the sponge around every inch of leather—twice—just to
make sure it was clean.

I dried everything and grabbed Charm's saddle pad to throw into the stable washing machine with a few other blankets that were inside. I'd pick it up tomorrow.

Satisfied with Charm's gleaming tack, I washed my hands and picked up my stuff. I walked back to my room feeling relaxed because I knew Paige was out. There wouldn't be any questions or looks.

After I showered and changed into jeans and an old, comfy T-shirt, our room felt tiny. I wanted to get out and study somewhere else. The Winchester common room would def be a mistake. Jas would probably be there, or at least someone else who thought I was a backstabbing boyfriend stealer. I wanted drama-free study time.

The media center seemed like a safe place. There were tons of rooms and I knew the least popular ones where none of my friends—or, I guess, former friends—would go. I loaded my book bag and walked across campus, taking the shortest route to the center. I was tired after my lesson and I didn't feel like trekking all over campus.

Inside, I hurried through the main lobby—ignoring the clumps of people who were trying to decide whether or not to watch a movie or grab one of the many flat screens and watch TV or a DVD.

I walked down a few different hallways, turning so

many times that I'd probably need a GPS to get out, until I found one of the rooms in the back that had no TV and was strictly for studying. I pushed open the door—glad to find it empty.

I spread my notebooks, homework assignment sheets, and pens on the table. I started with math and got through fifteen out of thirty problems before needing a break. My calendar was open in front of me and I started filling each slot with what I needed to do each day from school to homework to riding. Every space for the next week was full— and I'd written in my tiniest handwriting. The squares were crowded with *Write paper, Do sci problems, Ride 1 hr,* and everything else that had to be done.

I checked the time on my phone. I'd spent an hour just *scheduling* my to-do list! I closed the calendar and shoved it to the side. I pulled out my syllabus for history, a class I was caught up in, and scanned the sheet for the next big assignment. We had an essay on the topic of our choice about European exploration. I flipped through my book for that chapter and started reading, determined to find an essay topic and get started early on the paper.

My phone buzzed. *When do u want the egg?* Jacob.

I wanted to text back *Never! U keep it!* But instead, I wrote, *2mrw @ hist class.*

I shut off the phone and went back to studying. I turned a page and tried to block out the laughter that was coming down the hallway. The door opened and Eric, Rachel, and her friends, plus Ben, Julia, and Troy walked inside.

Rachel's eyes met mine for a second before she looked away. She was the only one to look at me except for Julia, who only glanced in my direction before sitting beside Ben.

Eric sat a few chairs away from me and Rachel took the seat next to him. Eric was wearing one of my fave shirts—a blue cotton T-shirt that was snuggly whenever I'd leaned into him.

Thinking about him started to make me sad, but I pushed it away. He could sit with Rachel if he wanted. We weren't together.

No one said a word—everyone just started working. The silence in the room was deafening in that weird way and I wished I'd picked a room with a TV just to have some sort of background noise. I didn't want to sit here with them—they were probably waiting for me to leave so they could talk about me. But if I got up and left now, it would look like they'd chased me out of the room. I had to keep pretending that I didn't care and was fine.

So I went back to work, forcing myself to stay. I still couldn't believe they'd picked *this* room. Out of every other room they could have chosen—it had to be this one. And the entire time, no one talked—everyone worked on homework. I kept sneaking glances at the wall clock.

Julia, sitting by Ben, looked over at me for a second and her mouth opened, then she closed it. And that was my cue to leave before she started grilling me about why I was here. I didn't look at anyone as I put away my stuff and slung my book bag over my shoulder. Troy was the only one to look up and give me a half smile.

I left and went down a side hallway. I walked by one of the TV rooms that was empty and had the door open. I halted mid-step and went back to look inside. This was *the* room. The couch. The TV. The place where Jacob and I had met for our first viewing of our documentary, *Horse Sense*. I'd been so nervous to sit next to Jacob on the couch—I'd almost jumped up when his arm had brushed mine. The memory made me smile.

When we'd filmed the movie at the stable, Jacob had acted weird the entire time. While I'd held Charm, Jacob had stayed as far away from me as possible. He'd left the second we'd finished filming and I'd been crushed. I'd thought it was because he'd stopped liking me or was

into someone else. I'd had *no* idea it was because he was afraid of horses. Jacob had gone along with my idea for *me* because he knew how much I loved horses. It was one of the sweetest things anyone had ever done for me. I stood in the doorway for a long, long time thinking about good memories and how quickly things can change.

8

THE NEW
BAD GIRL

WHEN I GOT BACK TO WINCHESTER, I WAITED
for the feeling of security, of being in my own dorm and
away from everyone, to wash over me. But it didn't. Instead,
I just felt annoyed at seeing Homecoming posters every
five feet.

"Sasha?" Livvie, my dorm monitor, called. She stepped
outside her office and I turned back to face her.

"Yeah?"

"Come in here a sec. I want to chat." Livvie waved her
arm in front of her, motioning for me to walk into her
office.

I did and she closed the door behind us.

"Sit, sit," Livvie said. She brushed her long brown
hair back and sat behind her giant wooden desk. It was

freakishly organized. Like, down to the paper clip collection. But that was Livvie.

I sat, trying to think if I was in trouble. My grades were fine—great, actually. I hadn't missed a class and I couldn't think of one reason for Livvie to call me in here.

Livvie smiled. "You're not in trouble," she said, as if reading my mind.

"Phew," I said. "I thought something was wrong."

Livvie looked down at her desktop calendar, then back at me. "Well, I'm hoping there isn't. Sash, Paige mentioned to me that you broke up with Eric. She said that you and Callie are going through a rough time. I'm sorry to hear that and please know that Paige only told me because she's worried about you."

I shook my head—I wasn't mad at Paige. "Worried how?"

"Worried that you're overextending yourself. Studying and riding all of the time. I'm *all* for working hard," Livvie said. "But you've got to take a break every once in a while. Your grades are wonderful, Mr. Conner tells me you're doing great at the stable, and none of your teachers have a single complaint."

"That's because I've been working so hard," I said. "Paige was right—I don't have a boyfriend and I lost one of my best friends. That left me with a lot of free time. So, I've been studying more and riding."

Livvie folded her hands on top of her desk. "But you realize that you can do other things with the free time besides work, right? You and Paige used to be the queens of DVDs and TV shows. I hope you're still making time for that."

"Oh, we are," I said. "For sure. And I'm fine—really. I'd come to you if I needed to talk."

I knew that's what Livvie needed to hear to let me out of her office. "Good," she said, smiling. "My door's always open. You can talk to me anytime."

I got up and flashed her a smile. "Thanks. I will."

Once I was outside of her office, I changed plans. I didn't feel like going back to my room just yet. Paige would be there with questions—ones I wouldn't answer. I decided to risk the common room even though running into Jasmine was likely.

Inside the cozy room, I grabbed a root beer from the fridge and a mini-pack of pretzels. I put my bag on the carpet and plopped beside it. I pulled out a notebook and wrote *things 2 do w/Charm* at the top. There were so many exercises we needed to practice before Mr. Conner taped a lesson for Mr. Nicholson.

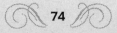

I munched on a pretzel and wrote *serpentines, shoulder-ins, transitions* on the piece of paper. The list kept growing down the page. Each item I added made me panicky. These were all things Charm and I had to do before next week.

So. Many. Things. I squinted, trying not to take in the whole list as I added the final entries. But the familiar feeling of nausea gripped me. It had held me captive the entire time I'd been lying about Jacob to Callie and Eric. And now it was back because I was nervous about not being able to get all of this done.

You'll start first thing tomorrow morning, I told myself. I'd be fine. Completely fine.

I glanced up when the common room door opened. Jasmine, groaning, walked inside. She came over and sat on the couch across from me. From my position on the floor, I knew she could see my list. I flipped to a clean sheet of paper.

"In a sad way, I'm kind of impressed by you, Sasha," Jas said.

I didn't even want to guess where this was going. "What are you even talking about, Jas? I'm busy."

Jas rolled her eyes. "Sure you are. No boyfriend. No best friend. Yeah, I'm sure your calendar is full." She put a hand over her heart, pausing for a second. "I just didn't know that you had it in you to do something like *that*. And to your best friend. It's kind of ironic, isn't it?"

I just stared at her. I'd learned it was better not to answer her rhetorical questions.

"I mean," Jasmine continued, "you, Callie, and Paige always looked at me as the bad girl. The horrible one who did mean, awful things. Look in the mirror now."

I forced myself not to react. Jasmine knew nothing. Not why I'd done anything that I had. She was so wrong.

Jas watched me for a few seconds, waiting for a reaction, then shrugged. "Whatever. I've got *friends* to go hang out with."

"Have fun," I said in an ubercheery voice.

Jasmine got up, walked over to the door, and opened it. But she stopped in the doorway and turned back to look at me. Her eyes focused on me and her dark hair swirled around her shoulders. "FYI, if being the new bad girl *is* what you want—don't even bother. I've done something way worse than anything you've done or could ever think up. So don't even try."

The door slammed behind her and I went back to my homework. I had an essay to write for history, so I started outlining it on paper. No way I was handwriting it, but I wasn't about to go to my room for my laptop.

I scribbled more notes and my eyelids started to feel heavy. I rested my forehead on my knee. *Two-minute nap and then back to work,* I told myself.

"Sasha?"

Someone's hand touched my shoulder and I felt a pen being taken from my fingers. I blinked and looked up at Paige.

"It's almost eleven," she said. "I've been waiting for you to come back for hours—I've been texting you nonstop."

"Oh, Paige, I'm sorry." I dug my phone out of my bag—it was on silent. "Is Livvie looking for me?"

"If you'd been in here much longer," Paige said. "I didn't tell her anything in case you just needed some time away from Winchester and I didn't want to get you in trouble. I had no idea you were in here. C'mon."

She held out a hand and pulled me up off the floor. She helped me gather my papers and shouldered my bag.

I didn't even remember changing clothes, washing my face or crawling into bed. I just knew I was out the second my head touched the pillow.

9

TEACHER'S PET

I WALKED INTO HISTORY CLASS—I'D BEEN dreading it from the second the day had begun. I had to take the egg and notebook from Jacob. I covered a yawn. After Paige had found me last night, we'd both gone to bed, but I'd gotten up at four thirty to finish homework and double-check my schedule.

Jacob was already in his seat when I slid into mine. He saw me, then leaned over and reached down beside his chair leg. He got up and walked over. Jacob held a box in one hand and the notebook in another.

He sat in the chair in front of me, turning around to face me.

"Hey," he said.

"Hi."

Awkward!

He put the box and notebook on my desk.

"I made the egg a cushion to keep it from breaking," Jacob said. He opened the top of the box lid, and inside, padded with cotton and Kleenex, was our egg. I peered at it.

"You drew a face on it," I said, trying not to laugh. "Omigod."

Jacob laughed. "Yeah, well, it needed it."

He'd drawn a goofy mouth, nose, eyes, and ears with a blue Sharpie on the egg.

"I love the eyes," I said, admiring the round eyes with tiny eyebrows.

"Thanks," Jacob said. "Since it's your egg too, you can draw something else on it if you want."

Jacob reached into his bag and pulled out a couple of different colored Sharpies.

"Okay."

I took a green one with a fine point and picked up the egg. I drew a sideways baseball hat on its head and wrote *CCA* on the hat.

"Niiice," Jacob said. "That's exactly what he needed."

"Excuse me? *He?*" I made a face at Jacob. "When was *that* decided?"

Jacob smiled. "It was obvious after I drew the face. I made him in blue and then you just added a baseball hat. Of course it's a boy egg."

"Oh, so a girl egg *definitely* wouldn't have a blue face or wear a hat?"

I reached over and swiped the blue Sharpie from Jacob.

"Sasha! What are you doing?" Jacob grabbed for the pen, but missed.

I giggled. "Careful! Don't break 'him.' And you forgot something."

Jacob shook his head, but watched as I started drawing on the egg.

"There," I said, holding it out to him. "Now what kind of egg is it?"

Jacob peered at it, then grinned. "I would guess that from the curly eyelashes you just gave *him*, it's now a girl."

"Exactly," I said. We smiled at each other, then I realized we were acting too friendly. Too close. This couldn't happen.

I sat back in my seat, creating more distance between us. "We can text tomorrow or something about when to trade again," I said. "I'll, um, log in our notebook that I took it now."

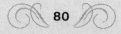

Jacob nodded—his smile fading. "Okay."

He went back to his seat and I snapped a pic of the egg on my desk. The rest of the classroom soon filled. I was so busy reading my to-do list, I didn't even notice Eric walk into the room. I just looked over and he was sitting in his seat.

Mr. Spellman walked into the room, smiling at us. "Before we get started," he said, "I want to remind everyone that group projects start at the end of next week and I hope you've all had a chance by now to be in contact with your partners and get to know each other."

I'd forgotten all about that. Mr. Spellman had put Jacob and Eric in the same group. I still didn't even know my group members—I'd have to ask Mr. Spellman who they were. I'd been in too much shock to pay attention after he'd said that Jacob and Eric would be partners.

"Let's talk about the reading," Mr. Spellman said. "Who wants to start our discussion?"

I raised my hand and Mr. Spellman nodded at me. I was beyond prepared for talking about the homework.

"I've read about the Industrial Revolution before," I said. "But I didn't remember how much it impacted society in such a huge way."

Mr. Spellman nodded. "Continue with that, Sasha."

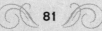

I talked for a few more minutes about how losing animal-driven power to machines had changed daily life for so many people. Mr. Spellman agreed with my answers and seemed pleased that I'd given such a detailed response.

And for the rest of class, I raised my hand every few questions. My participation grade was going to skyrocket after this class. Everyone already thought I was a back-stabbing boyfriend stealer, so who cared if they thought I was a teacher's pet, too?

10

SOMETHING REALLY INTERESTING

I LUGGED CHARM'S SADDLE DOWN THE AISLE—— it felt heavier than I remembered. Sweat was already prickling along the back of my neck and I was tired before the lesson had even started. At least it was the middle of the week—I'd have the entire weekend to tackle things on my list.

Charm, sensing my mood, was quiet while I tacked him up. We walked outside to the outdoor arena. Heather and Jasmine were already on horseback and trotting in figure eights. Thankfully, the early evening sun wasn't in our faces and the air was starting to cool.

I stuck my foot in the stirrup, hopping to keep my balance. That was lame! Mounting was so basic—I shouldn't have had one second of a misstep. I looked up to see if Heather or Jas had noticed, but they were too focused to even care what I was doing. I mounted and gave Charm rein to move into a walk. He stretched his neck and ambled toward the fence.

We'd just finished warming up when Mr. Conner came into the arena. "Ready to work over jumps today?" he asked us.

We nodded.

"Good," Mr. Conner said. "If all of your horses are warmed up, then you'll each take turns jumping the three verticals and two oxers that are arranged at the other end of the arena. Jasmine, you'll ride first."

Jas tapped her heels against Phoenix's side and the gelding moved easily from a walk to a collected trot. Jasmine circled him once and then urged him toward the first jump. Phoenix, a total pro, sailed over the first three-foot high vertical and stayed focused as Jas took him over the next two verticals and the oxers. Jasmine had finally taken Mr. Conner's warnings seriously that he wasn't going to tolerate her pushing Phoenix over every jump. She'd made a noticeable effort to become a softer rider and it showed.

Phoenix gathered himself before the last oxer, preparing for the spread, and surged into the air. He cleared it and Jas patted his neck once—a rare sign of affection from her.

"Excellent," Mr. Conner said. "You were quiet and Phoenix stayed focused. You continue to impress me with your efforts to relax with Phoenix. It showed on these jumps. Please keep it up."

Jasmine grinned. "Thanks."

"Sasha, you can start whenever you're ready," Mr. Conner said.

I nodded and gathered the reins. I dropped my hands and sat deeper in the saddle, urging Charm into a trot. He bounded forward and I let him go to the first vertical. He rocked back on his haunches, tucked his knees, and cleared the rails. Six strides later, we reached the second vertical—this one a couple of inches higher with flower boxes on the sides. Charm approached the jump, pointed his ears forward, and launched into the air. He hit the ground a little harder than he should have and it made me wobble in the saddle. I was being ridiculous—first with the mounting and now this? I had to start going to the gym.

We cleared the final jumps and Charm tossed his head, proud of how he'd done. I patted his neck and stopped him beside Aristocrat.

Mr. Conner looked at me, smiling. "Nice ride, Sasha. You recovered your balance after losing it on

that vertical and it didn't affect the rest of the jumps. Good effort."

I settled into the saddle, glad to be finished with my ride. Heather went next and Aristocrat took each three-foot jump as if it was tiny. He jumped without much effort and Heather stayed relaxed but solid in the saddle. I watched how focused she was and wished I could channel more of that.

Mr. Conner praised her ride, then asked us to take the course in reverse. When it was my turn again, Charm and I made it easily over the first oxer. He cantered toward the second jump and I signaled him to take off too late. Charm hit the rail with his knees and it tumbled to the ground. My face burned with embarrassment, but I didn't lose focus and we had a good ride for the rest of the round.

Heather and Jasmine both jumped the course clean. Jasmine's ride was particularly strong. She looked as if she'd ridden the course a million times and didn't have to even think about the jumps. She was a consistent rider, which was something crucial to staying on the YENT. It was also something Charm and I didn't have yet.

"Nice work, everyone," Mr. Conner said. "See you tomorrow."

I dismounted and my knees shook a little as I loosened Charm's girth and led him out of the arena. I really had to start working out more—this was ridiculous. I'd known Mr. Conner's YENT lessons were going to be rigorous and I had to be better prepared to handle them.

I led Charm away from Jasmine and Heather and we went to a deserted grassy lane near one of the big pastures. Horses dotted the field and some, far up on the hill, looked like specks of black, brown, and gray.

Charm seemed to like the change of scenery and he ambled quietly beside me. The sun was just starting to set and it dipped behind a cluster of trees at the far edge of campus.

"Things are kind of tough right now," I confessed to Charm. He flicked an ear at me. "I don't want Eric back— I hurt him too much—and I'm glad Jacob stayed with Callie. But . . . I'm on my own. I've got Paige, but she just won't stop asking about everything I don't want to talk about."

Charm seemed to listen and take in my words.

"I hate being in my room because I can't stand looking at Paige's face when I keep refusing to answer any of her questions. And the common room isn't much better because Jasmine always manages to show up."

I fell silent, lost in my thoughts until I saw Alison jogging my way with Sunstruck, her palomino gelding, trotting beside her. The Arabian's neck was arched. I could watch him move all day. There was a lightness and spring to every one of his moves that Charm, a Thoroughbred/ Belgian mix, couldn't replicate.

"Hey," Alison said. She slowed Sunstruck to a walk, the gold chain links jangling on his brown leather lead line. Alison's face was pink and she was sweating, even in shorts and a tank top.

"So you're working him over the lanes, huh?" I asked.

Alison patted his neck and turned Sunstruck to follow Charm and me. "Yeah. Mr. Conner loved your idea—he thought it was a great way for me to keep my bond with Sunstruck and for both of us to work out together."

"I know it's not even close to riding," I said. "But Sunstruck just wants to spend time with you—no matter what you're doing."

Alison nodded. "You're right. He's been an angel the entire time."

We walked the horses, silent, for a few minutes.

"So, how are you doing with . . . things?" Alison asked, her voice soft.

I took a long, deep breath. I had nothing to lose by

talking to her. "Honestly? Not so great. Callie. Eric. Jacob. The whole thing's just a mess. And Jas has been her usual charming self and I feel like she's stalking me in Winchester."

Alison frowned. "I'm sorry. That's not fun. It's enough to deal with what happened, and of course she's in your face."

I looked at Alison. "But she did say something really interesting. We were in the common room and she accused me of trying to be the new 'bad girl' on campus."

Alison scrunched her nose. "Why? Because of the Jacob thing?"

"Yeah." I wanted to move past that part of the convo ASAP. "But she said she'd already done something much worse than I'd done and could ever think up."

Alison sighed. "Julia would *kill* me for talking to you about this."

"Up to you, but who am I going to tell?" I asked. "I have zero friends except for Paige, and even that's weird right now."

"Well, I just *know* Jasmine's talking about what she did to Julia and me," Alison said. "She framed us. I know it. I'm *positive.* I don't know how, but I swear—Julia and I didn't cheat on our history exam. Jas did something and now she's bragging about it."

"She's too smart for that," I said. "Even if she did frame you—she's not stupid. She'd never brag about something that serious—she'd be expelled if she got caught."

"I never said she was stupid. Just cocky. She thinks she can do whatever she wants and get away it."

I hesitated. "If you're really sure she framed you, then you've got to get proof. You, Julia, and Heather are all smarter than she is—figure out something and get back on the team."

Alison nodded. "We will. Somehow, we will." She checked her watch. "I want to jog him another half mile before it gets dark. See you in English?"

"Okay, bye."

Alison turned Sunstruck back in the opposite direction and started jogging beside him. I led Charm down the lane and into the stable.

If Alison was telling the truth, then what Jas had said would make perfect sense.

II

FOR OUR
HEALTH CLASS

I WALKED INTO MY DORM ROOM, SMILING when I saw Paige typing on her computer and blushing.

"Let me guess," I said. "IMing with Ryan?"

Paige ducked her head. "Yeah. But he was just asking me if I wanted to eat breakfast together sometime."

"And you said yes, right?" I asked.

"I told him Friday would be fine."

I walked over and gave Paige a high five. "Perfect. You weren't like, 'Omigod, tomorrow!' You played it cool."

"You think?" Paige asked.

"Absolutely. That was great."

Paige closed her laptop. "How was your lesson? You look a little stressed or something."

"It was kind of tiring," I said. "But okay. I'm just gross and need to get cleaned up."

"I've got the perfect solution to make you feel better," Paige said, smiling. "A trip to the Sweet Shoppe. It *is* Wednesday, after all. I think they have new smoothie flavors."

I'd *really* missed hanging out with Paige. And things had been so weird that this would be the perfect chance for us to chat and relax.

"That sounds great," I said. And I didn't want to, but I had to say it. "I'm serious, though, if you bring up the party—I'm going to leave. I really, really don't want to talk about it."

Paige half-shrugged. "Okay. I won't say a word."

"Give me fifteen minutes to shower and change, then I'm ready."

After I got cleaned up, we grabbed our purses and I picked up my egg box off my nightstand. I'd left it in my room while I'd been riding. Utz would never know and the stable was, like, the least safe place ever for an egg. I'd take a pic of it with me at the Sweet Shoppe. If I had to do this dumb assignment, I was *definitely* going to get an A.

"Ugh," Paige said as we stepped outside. "It's disgusting out here."

"Totally." We both pulled on our sunglasses.

"But at least we're going to be eating something amazing in five minutes," I said.

We walked the short distance to the Sweet Shoppe and with each step, our tension eased.

"My math teacher is trying to kill my class," Paige said.

I grinned. "What? How?"

Paige rolled her eyes. "Okay, get this: not only did he assign *fifty* homework problems for tonight, but he also told us we have a quiz on Friday and a test next week. During *Homecoming*. It's so wrong."

"That's ridiculous. But focus on Homecoming and fall break. Those are exciting."

As soon as I said "fall break," I wished I hadn't. I was staying with Paige in New York City, which had been perfect when we'd made the plans. Mom and Dad had agreed to let me go and then had decided to go on vacation while I was at Paige's. Now Paige's was only going to be fun if we fixed our shaky friendship.

"You're so right! Homecoming *and* fall break," Paige said. She almost bounced as she walked. "Forget about math. Those *are* awesome things to look forward to. We're going to have so much fun over break."

I nodded, glad that we were walking up the stairs to

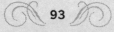

the Sweet Shoppe. I pulled open the door and stepped into the air-conditioned room. If Paige and I got through this without having any weirdness, then maybe she was finally taking me seriously about no party talk.

Paige and I both stared at the smoothie choices on the cute chalkboard hanging behind the counter. Colored chalk matched the drink flavor—so blueberry was written in blue, strawberry in red, and mango in orange. Everything about the Sweet Shoppe was fun—from the glass counter where we could see all of the ice cream tubs to the cupcake trees that were displayed on the counter with a zillion different choices.

"Oooh, so many!" Paige said. "Want to get two large ones, drink half, and swap?"

"Duh. I'm going to get peach mango."

Paige scanned the choices. "And I'll get . . . blackberry and strawberry."

"Awesome."

We stepped up to the counter and ordered our smoothies. The barista handed them to us and we found an empty circle-shaped table near the center of the shop. We sat and started sipping.

"So let's talk fall break," Paige said.

I took a huge gulp of smoothie and got a brain freeze.

Owww. "Yeah," I said. "It's going to be so much fun."

"There's so much we didn't get to do when you visited me over the summer," Paige said. "I mean, we stayed in Manhattan the entire time. There's *so* much more."

"Like what?" I asked. This felt right—Paige and me. No awkwardness. Just the two of us talking and enjoying our mid-week treat break.

"Like places that would horrify my mom if I told her we were going." Paige grinned.

"Tell me!"

"Well," Paige looked over her shoulder, as if expecting Mrs. Parker to suddenly appear. "A new train line started near my house. So . . . we tell my mom we're going shopping and instead, we should sneak off to Coney Island."

"*The* Coney Island? I've only seen that in pictures and movies. Omigod, that would be so cool."

Paige nodded. "Some of the rides might be closed, but I just want to see the park. My parents wouldn't take me and I've never been to Brooklyn."

"Well, we're going then. We'll tell your mom we're going to Saks or somewhere fancy and instead, we'll be eating cotton candy at Coney Island."

"We'll even get our own MetroCards for the subway," Paige said, sitting up straighter. "Like adults."

I smiled. "I want my own MetroCard. That sounds awesome. How many times have you ridden the subway?"

Paige frowned. "Only twice. Both times it was when my uncle from Philly came to visit. He thought I needed to experience it instead of taking a cab everywhere."

"Will we"—I paused—"get lost underground, Paige Parker?"

"No! Maybe! I don't know!" Paige said, giggling. "Hopefully not."

We laughed and swapped smoothies.

"If we do, I hope it's on the way home 'cause at least we'd have cotton candy to eat."

Paige took a drink. "Yeah, and—"

But her voice faded away when I saw Jacob walk past us and sit down. He had a frozen hot chocolate and as he sipped from his glass, I couldn't stop the flood of memories. I flashed back to when we'd had hot chocolate together last fall. I'd eaten all of my marshmallows before I'd finished my drink, so Jacob had spooned some of his into my cup.

"Um," I said to Paige. My voice sounded so *weird*. "Jacob's here and I . . . need to get a pic of us with our egg. For health. For class. For our health class."

"Okay," Paige said. She gave me a sideways look, but didn't say anything.

I reached into my purse for the egg and grabbed my phone. It was fine that I was going over to Jacob. Like I'd just told Paige, this was for class. And I wanted an A.

I stood and walked over to Jacob's table. I stopped beside him, looking at my pink flip-flops and then at him. "Hi," I said. "I brought the egg. Since we're both here, I thought we could get a pic of us with it."

Jacob nodded. "Hey, good idea." He pushed his drink to the side and held out a hand for the egg box. I handed it to him and he set it in front of him and opened it. He took out the egg and held it between his index finger and thumb so the face was visible.

"Okay," I said. I flipped open my phone and moved closer to Jacob's shoulder. I leaned down so both of our faces and the egg were in the shot. My finger fumbled for the camera button and the second I clicked it, Callie appeared in front of us.

"*What* are you doing?" she asked. Her gaze flicked from Jacob to me.

Immediately, I jumped away from him, almost dropping my phone. "Nothing. Just taking a picture of our egg for health class."

My voice rose with every word. I sounded *so* guilty!

Callie looked down at the egg and rolled her eyes. "Fine.

Are you done now? I came here to meet my *boyfriend*."

"We're done," I said. I started to apologize for making her upset, but I knew I couldn't. There couldn't be one crack in my I-really-did-try-to-steal-your-BF facade.

"You want to keep the egg for a while?" I asked Jacob.

"Sure," he said.

"I forgot the notebook, so just write wherever you take it on paper and I'll add it in," I said.

He nodded and I sidestepped Callie, hurrying back to my table with Paige. I felt Callie's glare burning into my back as I walked away. I sat across from Paige and gulped my smoothie to stop the flush in my cheeks.

"Let's go," Paige said.

We grabbed our plastic cups and walked out of the Sweet Shoppe. For once, I was glad Paige could read me so well. She just knew it was time to go.

"I've got to run over to Geena's for a sec," Paige said. "So, meet you back at Winchester?"

"Sure," I said. "See you later."

Paige and I split up and I started for Winchester, taking the prettiest route through the courtyard. I started to walk by the benches, but I felt so tired. What was my problem? I sat on one of the benches and drew up my legs, resting my chin on my knees. I closed my eyes for a second.

"Silver."

I looked up and Heather was staring at me—arms folded.

"What?" I asked.

"You've been a hot mess for days," Heather said.

"Wow," I said. "Thanks."

"So what's your deal?" Heather asked, an eyebrow raised.

"Just . . . tired," I said, honestly.

"Well, maybe it's time to take it easy."

"Whatever," I said. "I'm fine."

Heather sighed. "Clearly. Look, why don't you come sleep over with Julia, Alison, and me."

I almost fell off my bench.

"Not because we like you or because we're going to do some big dumb girly sleepover," Heather added quickly. "Just so you can relax. Just this once."

"So you do care," I teased.

Heather snorted. "Puh-lease. I just don't want to be alone with Jasmine if you get sick or something and have to skip a lesson. At least she focuses most of her attention on you." Heather gave me a sweet smile.

"Oh, nice," I said.

"Are you coming over or what?" Heather asked.

I was surprised when I didn't even pause. "Yeah, I think I will. I mean, I have to ask my dorm monitor, but if she says okay, I'll pack a bag."

"See you in, like, an hour?" Heather said. I nodded, not saying anything as she walked off.

I sat there for a second, stunned. *What* had just happened? And how was I going to explain to Paige that I was going to spend the night at the Trio's?

When I got back to Winchester, I paused in Livvie's doorway.

"Can I ask you something?" I asked.

"Sure," she said. "What's up?"

"I know it's a school night," I said, realizing that would be the first thing she'd question. "But I was wondering if I could go sleepover in Orchard. Just for one night. I . . . kind of need to get out of Winchester."

"Are you and Paige having problems?" Livvie asked.

"No," I said quickly. "It's just Jasmine. If I sleep over in Orchard with Heather, Julia, and Alison, I won't have to see her."

Livvie nodded slowly. She was probably thinking about my past with the Trio. "It's fine with me. But like you said it *is* a school night and you'd still have to follow the rules and go to bed on time."

"Promise," I said.

"Let me call Stephanie and see if it's okay with her," Livvie said.

I waited while she called Orchard's dorm monitor. When she hung up the phone a few minutes later, Livvie smiled. "It's fine with her. Have fun and relax a little, Sash. You've been working so hard lately."

"I will," I said. "I'll be back tomorrow morning before class."

Livvie nodded.

When I got to my room, Paige was already inside.

"That was fast," I said. I'd needed more time to work out my I'm-staying-with-the-Trio speech.

"Yeah, I just needed to grab a recipe from her," Paige said.

I walked over to my bed, trying to come up with what to say. But I had to say it—just get it over. There was no right way to tell Paige.

"So, about tonight . . . Heather invited me to sleep over in Orchard. You know, to get away from Jasmine and everything."

Paige stared at me as if it was a joke, like she was waiting for me to laugh and tell her I was just kidding.

"Oh," Paige said, sitting back in her chair. "If you think

that'll make you feel better, then you should definitely go. But are you *sure*? You can escape Jasmine by staying in our room. You don't have to stay with the Trio to get away from her."

"It's one night," I said guiltily. "I kind of just want to get out of Winchester. But not because of you." I added the last sentence quickly. "I know we'd have a great night, but you know how a change of scenery can help sometimes."

Paige blinked a few times, then smiled. She was trying to make me think she was okay, but I could tell she probably wasn't. I'd hurt her feelings. But I couldn't stay here. I *had* to get out of Winchester.

"It'll be good," she said, getting up. "You'll come back with tons of awesome stories about the Trio that we never knew."

"Exactly," I said. "I'll sneak into their bathroom to text you if something awesome happens."

I went to my closet to pack. I took out my pink bag with a silver star in the middle that was the perfect size for an overnight trip. Paige was at her desk working on homework—at least I'd gotten mine done in between classes.

My toothbrush, hairbrush, makeup, and other bathroom

stuff fit into a cute bag with anime kittens on it that I'd bought from Sephora a few weeks ago. I looked outside and saw it was starting to drizzle. I grabbed my umbrella and put on my shoes.

"So, I'm going to go," I said. "Maybe you could get Geena or someone to sleep over tonight. If Livvie's letting me go, she definitely wouldn't mind."

Paige smiled. "Yeah, maybe I will. Have fun with the . . . Trio."

I nodded. "I'll see you tomorrow."

I walked out of our door and hurried out of Winchester. *So* awkward! I knew poor Paige didn't understand why I was staying with the Trio and I was sure I'd made her feel bad, but I had to go. I stepped out of Winchester and stopped under the overhang. The drizzle had turned to a downpour.

I opened my purple mini-umbrella and walked down the sidewalk toward Orchard, not having a clue how tonight was going to unfold.

12

A CRITICAL
MOMENT

MY PACE SLOWED WITH EVERY STEP AS I walked toward Orchard. I tried to imagine what we'd talk about. There was no way Julia wanted me to sleep over. Alison would be nice to me, but she'd never be too friendly with me when Julia was around.

And then I stopped. I'd forgotten something. Something important. Orchard was *Callie's* dorm. What if I ran into her in the hallway?

I forced myself to keep walking. If I ran into Callie, I'd figure out what to do in the moment. I pulled open the glass door to Orchard and stepped into the hallway. I wiped my rain boots on the doorway carpet and shook out my umbrella.

I walked down the main hallway, my shoes squeaking

on the glossy wooden floor. I climbed the stairs to the second floor where Julia, Alison, and Heather lived. Last semester, Julia and Alison had roomed together and Heather had a roommate I'd never met. This semester, the girls had managed to wrangle a triple and they'd all moved in together. Over summer break, Paige and I had talked about asking Callie to apply for a triple with us in Winchester, but we'd decided not to at the last minute because we liked how things were. Now I was *so* glad we hadn't asked Callie to move in with us.

I stopped in front of the last door on the second floor and my hand hovered in the air. I'd never slept over in anyone else's room other than Callie's. I hoped the entire night wouldn't be weird.

I knocked on the door and Alison opened it. "Hey," she said. "C'mon in." She ushered me inside.

OMG.

I almost froze in the doorway.

Their suite was *gorgeous*. They actually had a small living room and three doors that led to separate bedrooms. The living room walls were a fresh off-white and two black pole lamps cast a soft yellow light over the room. There was a square espresso-colored coffee table in the center of the room, directly in front of a flat screen TV mounted on the wall. The entire room was covered in thick, lush, dark brown carpet. And as if that wasn't enough, there was a tiny kitchen area with a counter, mini-fridge, and a microwave.

Paige and I were obviously living in the wrong dorm.

"You guys each have your *own* room?" I asked.

Alison nodded. "Yeah. Heather must have pulled some strings to get us in. I think they're really meant for high school students. But isn't it insane? I'm still not used to having my own room after sharing with Julia last year."

I glanced around, still taking in their suite. Black-and-white photos of the NYC skyline, a park, and a horse made the room feel sophisticated.

"Want a tour?" Alison asked.

"Uh, yeah!" I said. "But where are Julia and Heather? Did they change their minds?" I was only half-joking. I shifted my bag over my shoulder.

Alison grinned. "No, they're getting snacks in the common room. They'll be here in a sec."

I followed Alison to the bedroom on the far right. "That's Heather's room," Alison said.

I peered through the doorway. Heather's room was gorgeous. White, round paper lanterns hung from the

ceiling, her platform bed had built-in drawers on the side
and her comforter was dark brown with white stripes. She
had photobox frames on the walls and they had oversized
pictures of the Trio, Heather standing in front of a castle
somewhere and Aristocrat. She had a bedside table with a
clear lamp with a soft pink shade. A docking station was
plugged in and charging her pink iPod. Her desk had a
black halogen lamp, a Mac that was in sleep mode, and a
stack of papers and textbooks.

"Cool," I said. "I love her room."

I'd imagined before what Heather's room might be
like, but had never known it would be so pretty, clean, and
simple. I'd pictured it like a queen's bedroom—very royal
and pretentious.

I stepped out of the doorway and walked to the next
room.

"This is Julia's," Alison said. "Cute, huh?"

Julia's taste was so different from Heather's. Her bed
had wicker baskets tucked underneath. Her bedspread,
white with flowers bursting with bright colors, made the
room feel cheery. Her desk chair was purple and her rug
was striped with a zillion fun colors. A giant heart poster
hung over her desk.

Hanging from the edge of her closet, though, were

four complete outfits. The hangers even had bracelets, a necklace, or a pair of earrings attached.

"Is Julia trying to find the right outfit for something?" I asked.

Alison shook her head. "Nope. She always picks out her clothes for the next four days in advance. It's her thing. She can't deal with choosing clothes the night before or in the morning. So, she watches the Weather Channel and figures it out."

"Wow," I said. "Never would have guessed that." I smiled to myself. "Her room is so cute."

Alison and I moved out of the doorway and walked a few steps.

"And finally," Alison said. "My room. You're staying with me, so I hope you like it."

Alison's walls were covered in her sketches and she had a stack of sketch books in one corner. She had art supplies—paints, paintbrushes, pencils, markers, and chalks in a bin by her desk. Her comforter, lavender with no designs, set off deep purple pillows that matched her rug. She had a whiteboard above her desk and in neon dry-erase markers, she'd written a couple of notes to herself— *Get new pens, Talk to math teacher abt ex credit.*

"Your room is amazing," I said, immediately noticing

her ladder bookcase. I walked over and looked. Every shelf was full of books—some were even stacked horizontal.

"You read a lot, huh?" I asked.

Alison nodded. "Yeah, I guess. Heather and Julia keep joking that I'm going to fill my entire room with books. I've got more in plastic bins under my bed."

I grinned. "My room at home is like that. I had the worst time picking my fave books to bring."

"Because even though the library has everything, there's something different about reading *your* copy," Alison said.

"Ex-actly," I said. "I knew I couldn't come to school without *National Velvet* and *My Friend Flicka*. Best horse classics."

Alison reached over and plucked a book from her shelf. "I just got this one over the summer and I've read it a million times already." She handed it to me.

"Omigod. The cover is *pink*," I said. "I love it already." The title, *Dork Diaries*, had a supercute smiley face in the *O* in *Dork*.

"It's only my new favorite book," Alison said. "It's a graphic novel about this girl, Nikki, and how she tries to fit in at her new school."

I flipped through the book, smiling at the adorable

drawings and the diary format of the book. Nikki seemed a lot like me during my first year at Canterwood—trying to fit in and find a place at a new school.

"I'm going to get this," I said. "It looks awesome."

Just as I handed the book back to Alison, the main door opened. I put down my bag and Alison and I walked into the living room. Julia and Heather stood there looking at me. I smiled at both of them—trying not to let them see how nervous I was. I sat down at the far end on their sand-colored couch and tried to stop my stomach from swirling.

Julia set down four cans of Coke on the coffee table and stared at me.

"That's *my* seat," Julia said.

"Oh," I said, jumping up. "Sorry."

"This is not happening all night," Heather said, shooting a glare at Julia. She put down a tray of snacks— pretzels, yogurt-covered raisins, grapes, and Cheez-Its. "Sasha's staying here—*deal* and stop the comments." She turned to me. "Sit."

I sat and Julia knew better than to argue with Heather. She plopped onto the opposite end of the couch and folded her arms.

"Your suite is awesome," I said.

Heather nodded. "Duh. Like we'd live anywhere that wasn't this cool. So, I vote that we order pizza, watch TV, and save the snacks for later tonight," Heather said.

I nodded. "Fine with me."

Julia nodded and started dialing on her cell phone. "Half cheese, half pepperoni?" she asked.

Everyone nodded and she placed the order. When Julia hung up the phone, we all kind of avoided eye contact. Maybe I'd made a mistake. I could be hanging with Paige right now, watching a DVD or something. I reached into my pocket and pulled out my current obsession—Lip Burst in juicy watermelon. I took my time applying a coat of the clear gloss and waited for someone to say something.

"Let's start watching something while we wait for the pizza," Heather said. "I just got the latest season of *Carrington Heights* on DVD. It's ridiculous that they don't offer that channel at school."

"Oooh, yesss!" Alison said. "I forgot about that. There weren't even any reruns on this summer. So rude. Put it on right now!"

"You probably haven't seen it before, but you'll figure it out," Julia told me.

"Actually, I own all of the other seasons except for this one." I grabbed a soda.

Julia mashed her lips together and didn't say anything.

Heather put in the DVD and we all focused on the TV. Soon, everyone's attention was on the teen drama. We jumped when someone knocked on the door. It was Stephanie, Orchard's dorm monitor. Delivery guys weren't allowed to come to our rooms, so he'd brought the order to her office.

"Hi, Sasha," Stephanie said, smiling at me. She was short and sweet-looking with shoulder-length light brown hair that hung in loose waves.

"Hi," I said, remembering that I'd first met her before when I'd been at Orchard with Callie.

Stephanie handed over the pizza to Alison and waved as she left. "Enjoy, girls!"

Julia grabbed a handful of napkins and four paper plates. We all sat around the coffee table. Heather opened the steaming box and each of us grabbed a slice. Alison hit play and we watched the DVD while devouring the pizza.

"So. Good," Alison said, her mouth full. "I looove pizza."

"Alison!" Julia said. "Watch it—don't get crumbs on the carpet. I just vacuumed yesterday."

"Sorry," Alison said. She leaned carefully over her plate.

In seconds, we were absorbed in the show again.

"Can you believe that Cristian left Miranda for Zoe?" Julia asked.

"Shhh," Alison said. "This. Is. A. Critical. Moment."

Julia and I actually traded grins and watched Alison lean closer to the TV. Soon, there was nothing left but pizza crusts. I had almost forgotten that I was with the Trio—it felt just like watching TV with Paige. The mood was relaxed and the weirdness from earlier had slipped away.

After we finished a disc of *Carrington Heights*, Alison turned to all of us. "I know this is clichéd and whatever, but want to do our nails? My sister got me a gift certificate to Sephora and I bought tons of nail polish."

We all looked at our nails—they were bare, jagged, and gross from being in the stable all of the time.

"I think we kind of have to," Julia said. "Mine are a mess."

"Mine too," I said.

"Let's do pj's first," Alison said. "Then we're cozy and ready for tonight."

Alison and I walked to her room and Julia and Heather

went to their rooms. Alison and I changed into our pajamas. I'd picked light blue pants with a matching T-shirt that had a cloud in the center. Alison had chosen purple leggings and an oversize gray T-shirt.

We walked into the living room and Julia and Heather soon joined us on the couch and recliner. Julia's pj's, a bright pink T-shirt that had matching shorts with white hearts, reminded me of the color scheme of her room.

Heather looked comfortable, but still perfect somehow, in black drawstring pants and a white tank top. I'd never seen any of them in pajamas before—just regular clothes or riding gear.

Alison went into the bathroom and came out with a lime green plastic container. She opened the lid and revealed dozens of bottles of polish, all lined up in the box.

"Wow," I said. "Awesome."

Alison looked through the polishes and pulled out a clear shade. "Base first," she said.

We took turns painting our nails, passing around the bottle when we were finished.

"Now the hard part," Julia said. "Choosing a color."

"I love this one," Heather said, picking up a light pink. "It's called 'Kiss on the Chic.' Cute."

"I'm feeling red," I said. "This is it—'Big Apple Red.'"

Julia and Alison picked their colors. Julia went with a dark purple and Alison chose a chocolate brown.

"Let's play a game," Heather said. "I vote for 'Versus.'"

"What's that?" I asked. "I've never heard of it."

"Oh, my cousin Joseph came up with it," Heather said. "It's easy. You pick two people you'd like to see go up against each other. Everyone else gets to ask you a question or two about the situation and circumstances. Then, you have to say why you think that person would win if they fought it out."

"It's *so* fun," Alison said. "Watch us play once and then you can come in on the next round."

"Okay," I said.

Heather came prepared. "Utz versus Headmistress Drake."

"Location?" Alison asked.

"Behind the admin building," Heather said.

"Situation?" Julia asked.

Heather paused, thinking. "Utz tackled a student because he broke one of her wrestling trophies."

"Already got it," Alison said. "Headmistress Drake would *so* win because even though Utz is a wrestler, the headmistress would be so furious that she'd take her down."

"Disagree," Julia said. "Utz would win because no matter how mad Drake was, Utz is a trained wrestler. Drake would have no chance against her."

Heather looked at both girls. "Both of you made good points, but I have to go with Drake. This is *her* school and if someone tackled a student, Drake could be sooo fired. So her anger at Utz would overcome her lack of training."

I loved this game!

"Alison, you go," Heather said.

"Okay, Violet versus Jasmine," Alison said.

"Who started it?" Heather asked.

"Violet," Alison said.

Julia leaned forward. "What are they fighting over?"

Alison took in a breath. "Um, whether or not Jasmine should tack up all of the Belles' horses before the next lesson."

"Did Jas do anything to make Violet mad?" I asked.

Alison shook her head. "Nope. Violet just told her to do it from now on."

We all sat back for a second, thinking about our answers.

"Violet," Heather said. "She's the leader of the Belles and Jas would do anything she says."

"Jas," Julia said. "She's barely willing to tack up Phoenix. There's no way she'd be that scared of Violet that she'd tack up three more horses."

I nodded. "Jas. She's not really hanging with the Belles that much anyway. Plus, Jas has gotten scary enough on her own—she doesn't need them anymore."

Alison looked at me. "I agree with Sasha. Jas would win. Julia, you go. Then Sasha."

Julia smirked at me and somehow I just knew I wasn't going to like her choices.

"Eric," she said, "versus Jacob."

"Where?" Alison asked.

"Eric's room in Blackwell," Julia said.

This was going to go *so* wrong. I could feel it.

"Did Eric invite Jacob over or did he just show up?" Heather asked.

"He showed up," Julia said.

I was going to ask the question before someone else did. "Why?"

"To fight over you because they both want you back," Julia said.

I took a breath and glanced down at my hands. They'd clenched and I hadn't even known it. I wasn't going to get up and leave. I could handle this.

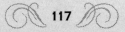

"Jacob," Alison said. "He does work out a lot."

Heather's eyes flickered to mine. "Jacob. He wants it more."

I sat, not wanting to answer.

"Hello?" Julia said. "Waiting."

"Jacob," I spat out. "Just because. I'm not giving a reason."

"Fine," Julia said. "And I picked him too. There's just something about the way he was acting for a while. Maybe he really does want you back."

We sat in silence as we finished our nails. I wondered if that meant something—we'd all disagreed on the previous answers, but Jacob had been the unchallenged winner of this round. Things were quiet for a few minutes before Alison and Julia started chatting. And I knew I just had to let go—it was a silly game and I'd come here to have fun. I wasn't going to spend the rest of the night analyzing why they'd all picked Jacob instead of at least one person choosing Eric.

We gossiped about the latest drama in our classes and they laughed when I told them about Utz's health class.

"I'd see how many times I could get away with breaking the egg before she was like, 'That's it! You're done,'" Heather said with a grin.

 **118**

"I was tempted," I said. "But Ja—" I stopped before I said his entire name, hoping they wouldn't notice.

"Ja—what?" Alison asked, looking up. "Ohhh." Her eyebrows shot up and she went back to painting her pinkie.

"Nothing. Jacob's my partner and he drew this really cute face on the egg, so I don't want to break it."

Julia stared at me as if she was about to stay something, but a look from Heather made her stop.

Someone's cell rang and Heather jumped up to answer it. "Hi, Dad," she said. She walked out of the living room and into her room, closing the door behind her.

Julia got up and went to the bathroom.

"Her dad calls *every* night," Alison said. "He wants a total progress report on what she worked on with Aristocrat. He freaks if she misses his call."

I glanced at Heather's door. "That's awful. She has to hate hearing her phone ring every night."

We both looked back at our nails when Julia emerged from the bathroom and Heather joined us seconds later.

"Everything okay?" Julia asked. I'd never heard such concern in her voice.

Heather nodded. "Yep. Just the usual."

Heather, using her unpainted hand, grabbed the remote and turned on a new episode.

13

FRIDAY NIGHT REVISITED

WHEN THE EPISODE ENDED AND THE CREDITS rolled, Heather left the DVD hovering on the menu. Our polish had dried and we each had shiny, pretty nails.

"Did you see Jasmine at all on your way out?" Heather asked me.

"Nope. I got lucky, I guess." I paused, trying to gauge how they'd react to my question. "So . . . have you guys come up with any evidence to prove Jas framed you?"

Heather, Julia, and Alison traded glances. Heather ate a green grape before looking up at me. "We haven't found anything yet."

"But we can't wait forever," Alison said. "Julia and I are going to *die* if we don't get to ride soon."

"I'd feel the same way," I said.

Julia shook her head. "We're miserable without riding."

And suddenly I believed them one hundred and ten percent. Both that they were unhappy and that they hadn't cheated. I still didn't trust Julia, or even Heather most of the time, but Alison and I had been getting closer. She really didn't seem like the kind of girl who would cheat.

"The longer we wait, the harder it's going to be," Heather said. "We've got to stop talking about it and do it."

"If I can help," I said. "I will. You can trust me. If Jas framed you, I want her to pay."

The Trio nodded.

"Thanks," Heather said after a minute. "We'll let you know."

Julia glanced at me for a second and for the first time, she didn't look as if she hated me. Her eyes weren't narrowed and she wasn't glaring at me. It was a normal glance.

We blew through a couple more episodes before my eyes started fluttering shut. Everyone else was quiet and Alison looked half-asleep already.

"I'm going to bed," Heather said.

"Me too," Julia said.

"And me," Alison added. "Steph was probably going to be at our door any minute anyway."

Heather flicked off the TV.

We stood, and tossed our pizza box and paper plates. Alison went into the bathroom and I was alone with Heather and Julia in the living room, waiting for my turn to wash my face and brush my teeth. I sank back onto the couch, fighting to keep my eyes open.

"Are you ever going to talk about the party?" Julia asked.

My heart started pounding and I tried to calm my breathing—maybe Julia would think I'd fallen asleep.

"Oh, please," Julia said. "I know you're not asleep. What happened?"

I opened my eyes and took a breath. "I came here to get away from all of that, not to talk about it. Okay?"

"So you're not going to say anything at all? You're hiding out here for a night and then you're going to go back and do what? Pretend nothing ever happened?" Julia pressed.

"Julia, drop it," Heather said. "We invited her over here to relax and you're not helping."

I smiled. Heather had a way of never being outright nice to me, but she'd just shielded me from Julia's questions. No one said anything as we took turns in the bathroom.

After I brushed my teeth and washed my face, I climbed into Alison's bed. Soon, I drifted off to sleep and smiled when I thought about how my obsession for lip gloss was almost rivaled by my new love of nail polish.

14

EARLY = RIDIC

THE NEXT MORNING, I OPENED MY EYES AND almost wasn't sure where I was. Then I remembered—I'd slept over in the Trio's suite. Talk about the ultimate never-saw-that-coming. The dials on Alison's clock changed to six thirty and tunes from the local pop station started playing. Alison reached over me and slapped the clock, falling back onto her pillow.

Five minutes later, the radio came back on and, with a growl, Alison pushed a button and sat up.

"I hate getting up so early," Alison said. "Ridic."

I sat up and ran my fingers through my tangled hair. "Agreed."

We got up and walked into the living room. Julia's door was still closed, but Heather was up and walking to her closet.

She pulled open the doors and I couldn't help but stare. Her clothing collection rivaled Paige's, but it wasn't the every-day clothes I was drooling over—it was the endless pairs of breeches, dozens of pairs of show boots and paddock boots, and crisp show shirts that filled half of the closet.

Julia's door opened and with her eyes half-closed, she walked to the bathroom, her fine hair staticky from the pillow.

Heather selected a dark purple polo shirt, pencil skirt, and ballet flats. Alison and I went back to her room, got dressed, and I started putting my stuff back in my bag. We met Heather in the living room.

"I'll just get cleaned up in my own room," I said. "Thanks for letting me sleep over."

Heather nodded. "Not that we're making a habit of it or anything, Silver."

"It was cool," Alison said, smiling.

"Tell Julia I said thanks," I said.

I picked up my bag and slid my feet into my flip-flops. Out in the hallway, I adjusted my bag and started down the hallway to the stairs. That had been *nothing* like I'd expected. Julia, Alison, and Heather had been cool most of the time and I'd had fun—a lot more fun than I'd ever thought.

I walked down the stairs and into the main hallway,

digging my phone out of my pocket. I wanted to text Paige to tell her I was on my way back and to see if I could gauge her mood. Not that she wouldn't be happy for me, but I knew she would still be hurt that I hadn't stayed in our room for the night.

"Sasha?" Callie walked over, one hand on her hip. "What are you doing here?"

I wanted to say *I miss you and I want our friendship back.* But instead, I shrugged. "I slept over."

Callie tilted her head. "Slept over *where?*"

"Here. With Julia, Alison, and Heather."

Callie threw her head back and smirked. "Wow. That didn't take long. I feel sorry for Paige. You already ditched her to sleep over with the Trio. Not like anything you'd do could shock me now, but still."

There was nothing else to say—nothing I *could* say. Everything about the way Callie was looking at me made me feel sick and I couldn't stand here another second. I stepped around her and left Orchard.

On my walk to Winchester, I started rethinking what to tell Paige. Did I tell her it was horrible? Fun? Boring? I hadn't texted her once all night—I'd completely forgotten about my phone, so maybe she'd guessed that nothing textworthy had really happened.

I reached my room and opened the door. Paige, standing in front of our full-length mirror, was brushing her hair.

"Hey," she said. She gave me a bright smile. "How was it?"

"It was *so* awkward at first," I said. "Alison was the only one in the suite when I got there and I could kind of tell that she was trying to be extra nice so that I didn't feel like trying to leave when Julia came and was mean to me."

"Uh-oh," Paige said. "Was she?"

I dropped my bag on the floor and sat cross-legged on my bed.

"At first," I said. "We watched TV and she made a couple of Julia-like comments, but whatever. I ignored her and things were okay."

"That's good," Paige said. "What else did you do?" She smoothed her blue pocket dress and put on silver ballet flats.

"We ate pizza while we watched TV and then we did our nails." I held out my hands for Paige's inspection.

"Oooh, pretty," she said. "I love that color."

"Me too. And that was it, really. We went to bed, got up, and I left while they were getting ready."

I'd purposely left out the part where I'd run into Callie. I didn't want Paige to be reminded of Friday at all.

"I'm glad you had fun," Paige said.

"Thanks. What did you do last night?"

Paige shook her head, laughing. "I was *so* lame. I put on a DVD and fell asleep! I woke up around midnight like, 'What's going on?' and for a second, I forgot where you were. Then, I remembered and fell back asleep."

I laughed. "At least you knew where I was."

Paige peered closer at me. "Did you guys stay up late? You still look tired, Sash."

"Not really," I said, defensively. "*I* don't think I look that tired."

Paige held up her hands. "Okay, sorry. I wasn't trying to insult you or anything. I'm just worried. You're doing a lot and I don't want you to get sick or something just because you don't want to slow down."

"I'm *not* going to get sick—I'm really okay."

I turned away from Paige and started getting ready for class. I caught a glimpse of myself in the mirror and saw faint purple circles under my eyes. I went into the bathroom and started applying concealer to the circles. Truth: I *was* tired, but I wasn't going to let it stop me from doing everything I needed to do. I was going to prove to Paige and everyone else that no matter how "tired" I looked, I could handle things.

15

ARE WE REALLY TALKING IN FRONT OF SASHA?

WHEN I SAT DOWN IN MATH CLASS, CALLIE was seated at the opposite side of the classroom and I stared at the whiteboard. Ms. Utz had already written today's homework assignments on the board. I'd had her for math last year and the class hadn't been too hard, but I still had to work at it to keep up my grade. The weirdest thing was having Utz for *two* classes this time. Heather walked into class seconds before it started, like usual.

"I'm going to pass back your quizzes from earlier in the week," Ms. Utz said. "Then, we'll go over last night's homework."

She passed back the papers, putting them facedown on our desks. She smiled at me when she reached my desk and put down my paper. From her smile, that was a definite A. I turned over the paper and saw a B+. A B+.

I counted how many problems there were and how many I'd gotten wrong. I fought the urge to slam my head into my desk. I'd been one right answer away from an A. One. Answer. I half-crumpled the paper and shoved it into my backpack. I'd studied for hours for that quiz. Utz should have just given me an F—that's what it felt like.

"Any questions about the quiz?" Ms. Utz asked.

I was half-tempted to raise my hand and ask how I'd studied so hard and only managed to pull a B+. But I didn't say anything.

"I'm still confused about how to solve problem six," Heather said.

"Okay," Ms. Utz said. "Everyone, look at number six and let's go through the steps. Heather, tell me how you started to answer it."

Heather told Utz how she started the problem and then Utz called on someone else to solve the next line. I tuned it out because, of course, that was a problem I'd gotten right.

It kind of surprised me to see Heather ask for help. She'd struggled with math last year and even though we hadn't been in the same class, I bet she'd asked as few

questions as possible. That was Heather's style—she was too embarrassed to look as if she didn't have the answer to everything.

But after that problem, I paid attention during every second of class and took a bunch of notes. If I wanted an A—I had to do more.

When it was time for lunch, I got in line and grabbed items that would only take minutes to eat so I could leave—a ham-and-cheese sandwich, applesauce, and a chocolate chip cookie. I started toward a table near the exit, when I saw Heather. She motioned to me and it felt as if everyone's eyes were on me again. Sitting with the Trio once was enough to cause everyone to talk, but this was going to make everyone freak.

I was as confused as they were that I'd been extended an invite back, especially after I'd just slept over.

I sat across from Julia, Heather, and Alison. We gave each other half smiles before we started eating. Julia took giant bites of her turkey-and-lettuce sandwich, and Alison had chosen mac and cheese with bacon bits and it smelled delicious. Heather had gone for veggie soup.

"Did you get a bad math grade?" Heather asked,

looking over at me. "You looked like you wanted to strangle Utz."

I took another bite before answering her. "I studied *so* hard and my grade was awful."

"You can get tutoring or something," Alison said. She pushed back her skinny black headband. "The semester just started."

"What'd you get, anyway?" Julia asked.

I leaned down, grabbed the mangled paper and handed it to her. I was too mad to be embarrassed.

Julia glanced at the paper, then started laughing. "You're serious. For real?"

"What?" Alison leaned over Julia's shoulder and looked. "A B+? You're upset about that?"

"I should have gotten an A."

Julia snorted and thrust the paper back at me. "If you'd gotten an F and you'd studied hard, you could have been upset. But not over a B+. That's just sad." Julia stood, shaking her head. "I'm going to get another soda."

Alison turned to me, her face full of sympathy. "A B+ isn't bad." She looked at Heather. "Want to see the drawing I spent all summer on that I got back today with a B in art class?"

Heather nodded. "Show me."

Alison pulled her art portfolio out of her bag and flipped through several drawings. I'd seen her horse sketches from last year and the ones in her room, but these were new and even better. Alison had lots of drawings of Sunstruck and I loved how proud the Arabian looked in some drawings and how gentle and calm he appeared in others. He was definitely hot-blooded, but he clicked with Alison and she knew just how to handle him.

Alison stopped on a page and turned the sketchbook sideways so both Heather and I could see. Three horses— Trix, Sunstruck, and Aristocrat—grazed in Canterwood's field. It was dusk outside and Alison must have spent hours shading every tree and fence rail to look as if the sun was hitting it just right.

"Alison, wow," I said. "*You* should be upset that you got a B on that. It's really, really amazing."

Heather nodded. "I agree. This is one of your best sketches. Did your teacher say why?"

Alison rolled her eyes. "She said I need to start 'expanding my options' and drawing other things besides horses."

"But you are, aren't you?" I asked. "Didn't you say you're working on a graphic novel?"

"Yeah, but it's about horses too," Alison said. "So my teacher will get mad if I submit it."

Heather sighed. "That's dumb. Can you sketch horse-related things? Like stables or riders or something?"

Alison sat up straighter. "Oooh, I haven't drawn people before. My teacher would love that—I could totally get away with it if I drew riders."

Heather, Alison, and I half-smiled at each other and I realized just how much one sleepover had kind of changed everything among all of us.

16

AIRBORNE

CLASSES FINALLY ENDED FOR THE DAY AND when I got to my room, I dropped off my stuff, changed, and headed for the stable. All day, I hadn't been able to shake the B+. I knew it was dumb and Alison was right—it *was* just a B+. But what if that B became a C? Or a D? Then, I'd go back to old Sasha from last fall—the girl who struggled with her grades.

That couldn't happen. I'd finally found my footing at Canterwood and I wasn't about to lose it. After this lesson, I'd go back to my room and study until lights-out.

I gathered Charm's tack, groomed him, and felt like I was going through the motions of tacking him up. I was on total autopilot. Not as if I needed to pay such close attention when tacking up a horse—I'd done it a thousand times—but I still needed to focus.

I tried to shake off the worries about grades and everything else going on and fastened my helmet. I felt a little dizzy and nauseous. But I was riding no matter what. I couldn't afford to skip even one lesson before Mr. Conner taped a class for Mr. Nicholson. Charm and I walked to the arena and I paused before I mounted. I took a long breath, squeezing my eyes shut for a second.

When I reopened them, the dizziness was gone. Phew. My stomach still felt gross, but maybe I'd eaten something bad at lunch. I mounted and started Charm in slow circles. Mr. Conner had set up the camera at the far side of the arena, so I walked Charm past it a few times. He didn't even look at it once. He loved having his picture taken, so I hadn't worried about him being freaked by the camera.

"Move, loser!" Jasmine said, cutting between Charm and the camera. She cantered Phoenix past us, and Charm, annoyed at Phoenix moving faster, tried to break into a canter. But I held him back to a walk. He fought me for a few seconds before listening.

"Is that as fast as you're going to warm up?" Jas asked, riding back over to us. She slowed and walked Phoenix by

Charm and me. "If that's true, then we won't be starting the lesson for hours while we wait for you."

"Omigod, *you're* not going to start at all if you don't stop talking because I'll make you want to leave the arena," Heather said, riding over to us.

I'd had enough. I let Charm into a trot and got him away from Jasmine and Heather. We warmed up without another word from Jasmine and I was glad when Mr. Conner finally entered the arena. All I wanted was for the lesson to be over so I could go back to my room and study. Maybe I'd ask Mike or Doug to cool and groom Charm for me just this once. I'd never asked them for a favor and I was sure they wouldn't mind.

"Hi, girls," Mr. Conner said. "If you're all ready, let's start with a sitting trot."

Heather, Jasmine, and I let our horses into trots. I sat to Charm's smooth gait and tried to keep my eyes between Charm's ears. It kept me from looking at Jas or Heather. I needed to stay focused on my riding and not think about anything else. But the B+ started nagging me again. *Stop,* I told myself. *You're going to study after riding.*

"Reverse directions," Mr. Conner said. I pressed my leg against Charm's side and guided him away from the wall.

We turned our horses and started them in the opposite direction. Charm felt a little stiff going this way, so I made a mental note to work with him more.

"Halt," Mr. Conner called. ·

Heather, Jasmine, and I brought our horses to halts.

"Trot," Mr. Conner said.

We let the horses move forward and within two strides, Charm was trotting. I posted and even though I knew Charm's trot was smooth, it made me feel nauseous as I posted.

Mr. Conner made us canter, work through a few circles, and then he held up a hand. "Bring your horses over," he said.

I rode Charm up to him and stopped. Rain was just starting to fall and it pinged lightly against the roof. It darkened outside by the second and it was my favorite kind of weather to curl up in bed with a book. Maybe I'd relax tonight and get up early and do my homework tomorrow.

What are you thinking? I argued with myself. I had tons of work to do. The fact that I'd even considered taking the night off was ridiculous. It had been bad enough that I'd spent the night before goofing off with the Trio when I should have been doing homework.

"We're going to take a few jumps," Mr. Conner said. "Heather, I want you to go first. There are two verticals and then a triple combination."

Heather nodded. "I'm ready."

She trotted Aristocrat toward the course and Jas and I followed at a walk. We stopped our horses next to Mr. Conner and we all watched as Heather urged Aristocrat forward and over the first vertical. He jumped it easily, not even looking at the blue-and-white rails. The second vertical, a couple of inches higher, didn't make him pause for a second.

Heather gathered him before the triple. They took the first jump, then two strides later Aristocrat launched into the air for the second. Their timing was perfect and Aristocrat was ready for the third obstacle. He jumped, landed cleanly, and Heather slowed him to a trot, then a walk. She rubbed a gloved hand down his neck and the dark chestnut arched his neck. He knew he'd done well.

"Collecting Aristocrat before the triple was exactly what you needed to do," Mr. Conner said. "Great job."

Heather smiled.

Mr. Conner nodded to Jasmine. "Go ahead."

Jasmine and Phoenix made it over the verticals without a problem. As she approached the triple, Jas gave Phoenix more rein and he rushed the first jump. The gray made it easily over the jump, but landed only a stride away from the second. He wasn't prepared to take off and neither was Jasmine. Phoenix jumped too late and his knees knocked the rail. His focus was broken and his ears flicked back and forth, waiting for a signal from Jas.

Instead of trying to steady him, she checked him to slow his stride to give both of them more time. But Phoenix was off. He made a huge effort to clear the last part of the triple, but this time his hind legs brought down the rail. They landed and I watched through one eye—afraid that Jasmine was going to yank him in a circle and make him take the course again.

But instead, she rode him back to us, her face red. If Mr. Conner hadn't been in the arena, she would have made Phoenix take the course a half dozen times after that round. But she knew better now—Mr. Conner wouldn't tolerate her rough handling of Phoenix.

"I don't have to tell you why he knocked two rails," Mr. Conner said. He looked at her expectantly.

Jasmine's eyes flickered to Heather and me, then she looked at Mr. Conner. "I gave him too much rein because I wanted to let him out more, but I should have kept him collected."

"I agree," Mr. Conner said. "Remember to keep working on not rushing him."

"I will," Jasmine said.

Mr. Conner looked at her for a second before turning to me. "Sasha, whenever you're ready, please begin."

I squeezed my legs against Charm's sides and urged him forward. He moved from a trot to a canter and we started toward the first vertical. I rose into the two-point position at just the right second and Charm cleared the jump. My legs shook a little on the landing and I tried to grip the saddle tighter with my knees. But my head started feeling weird again—like everything was rushing by me way too fast.

Charm's hoofbeats pounded in my ears. I grasped Charm's mane to keep my balance. *Just four more jumps*, I told myself. Then I would be done. Charm cantered to the second vertical and I swayed in the saddle, almost falling off the side. He leaped into the air and my hands slipped off his mane. His launch threw me backward and my fingers couldn't hold onto the reins. I felt like I was sailing through the air.

There was a thud.

And everything went black.

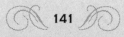

17

BLACKOUT

"SASHA? SASHA?"

My eyes fluttered opened and dozens of black spots swam in front of my eyes as I stared at the ceiling of the indoor arena.

I shifted my gaze and Mr. Conner, Heather, and Jasmine were kneeling beside me. I'd never seen Jasmine look like that—worried. Her eyes were open wide and she'd lost the color from her face. Heather's fingers were shaking as she held her cell up to her ear.

"Don't move, Sasha," Mr. Conner said. "Heather's calling the nurse."

I sucked in a breath—the wind had been knocked out of me, but I didn't think I was hurt.

Jasmine looked down at me. She started to touch my

arm, then pulled back her hand. "Um, want me to take off your helmet or something?"

"No, thanks," I said. I eased up on my elbows, undid my chin strap, and put my helmet beside me. "I'm fine, really. I just got dizzy and fainted, I guess. No big deal."

Mr. Conner touched my arm. "Sasha, it *is* a big deal. Don't get up yet. Does anything feel broken or sprained?"

I moved my arms and legs. "No," I said. "I'm fine." Mr. Conner watched as I rolled my shoulders and tilted my head from side. Jasmine disappeared and came back a few minutes later with a soda. She handed it to me.

"Thanks," I said. I sipped it and the bubbles made my stomach feel better.

"I promise that I'm okay," I said to Mr. Conner. "Really, I was feeling sick before the lesson and I shouldn't have ridden, but I did. Is Charm okay? Where is he?" I looked around and Doug held Phoenix and Aristocrat by the exit, but Charm was gone.

"Mike took him to cool him out and put him away," Mr. Conner said. "He's completely fine."

Phew. At least Charm wasn't hurt because I'd been dumb enough to ride when I'd been sick.

"The nurse is expecting Sasha," Heather said, closing her phone. "I can walk her over when she's ready."

I didn't have time to see the nurse. There were a million things to do on my list. "I don't need to see the nurse," I said. I started to stand and Mr. Conner grabbed my elbow, helping me up.

"Sasha," he said, frowning. "This isn't optional. Either I'll walk you over or Heather will."

"I'm—" I started to protest, but the look on his face told me I had no choice.

"Let's go," Heather said. "Do you want to sit at the stable for a while or go over now?"

Ugh! She wasn't going to let me out of this either.

"Let's go now," I grumbled. I took a couple of steps and the spots faded. I took another drink and Heather walked close to me, like she was afraid I was going to faint again. "I'm fine, really."

"If you're gonna pass out, at least aim for the grass and not the sidewalk," Heather said. "I'm not catching you."

That made me smile. "Deal." At least it had stopped raining when we stepped outside—everything was slick and the sky was still gray.

Heather and I walked down the sidewalk to the infirmary. Heather pulled open the door for me and pointed to a hard plastic chair. "Sit. You're walking at snail speed, so let me go sign you in."

I rolled my eyes, but sat down. Heather actually cared. Just a tiny bit.

Heather told the receptionist I was here, then sat beside me.

"You can go," I said. "I'm *fine*."

Heather pulled out her phone and started texting. "Like I *want* to be here? But if I leave and you pass out in your chair or something, Mr. Conner will blame me. So shut up and just sit there, fainter."

We waited for a few minutes before a nurse in blue scrubs walked over with a chart in her hand. "Sasha, come with me and we'll get you checked out."

"Okay." I got up and looked back at Heather.

She sighed. "I'm staying till you get back. Get over it."

I hid my smile and followed the nurse. I already felt so much better in the AC and the soda had made my stomach less queasy.

She took my height, weight, blood pressure, and all of that normal stuff. She asked me a ton of questions about what I'd been eating, drinking, and what my schedule had been like. After a few more tests, she finished marking on her chart and looked up at me.

"You're suffering from mild dehydration and exhaustion," she said. "I want you to go back to your dorm room and slowly drink a few glasses of water. And rest. I'm going to give you an excuse from classes tomorrow. You need a day to recover. Keep drinking fluids. That should make you feel better. And if there are ways for you to slow down your schedule, please try."

"Okay," I said. "But can I go to my riding lesson tomorrow? I really can't miss it."

The nurse shook her head. "I don't think that's wise. I want you to rest the *entire* day. If you still feel dizzy tomorrow, you need to come back, all right?"

"I will," I said. "Thanks."

The nurse wrote something in illegible handwriting and handed me a tiny slip of paper. "Give that to the receptionist for your excuse from classes. Feel better and please call us if you don't."

I smiled at her and walked out of the room. I opened the door to the waiting room and saw Heather still sitting where I'd left her. And pacing by the door was Jacob.

His hands were jammed in his front pockets and his eyebrows were pushed together. He and Heather both looked up at me at the same second.

"Sasha," Jacob said, walking over to me. "I heard that you fainted. Are you okay? What's wrong?"

Heather was off her chair and between us in two

strides. "Calm down, Jacob. God, you're going to make her faint just by being in her face."

"I'm *fine*," I said, trying not to look at Jacob and just concentrating on Heather. "Just mild exhaustion and I need to drink water or something."

I stepped around them and handed the note to the receptionist.

"You sure?" Jacob asked, his green eyes moving back and forth over my face.

"I'm sure."

The receptionist handed me back a note. "You're excused from all classes tomorrow," she said. "Take it easy."

I smiled my thanks and Heather, still between Jacob and me, turned to him. "You can go now," she said. "Sasha's okay."

Jacob didn't want to leave. I could see it in his face. "I . . . hope you feel better, Sash. You can always text—"

I shook my head. We both knew better. His eyes lingered on my face for a second, then he walked out of the infirmary.

Heather looked at me with a knowing glance, but didn't say anything. "I'll walk you back to Winchester," she said.

18

I'M FINE,
SERIOUSLY!

WHEN HEATHER LEFT ME AT THE STEPS OF Winchester, Livvie was there and waiting. She took my arm and led me into her office.

"Sasha," Livvie said. Lines of worry showed on her forehead and she looked stressed. She held my arm as I sat down and then went to sit behind her desk. "I got a call from the infirmary that you fainted during your lesson. How are you feeling now?"

"Much better," I said. "I didn't drink enough water and I was overtired. But I'm going to rest and I'll be fine."

"Well, I'm going to make sure dinner is delivered to your room tonight. I'll check on you tomorrow since you're excused from classes," Livvie said.

"Thanks," I said.

"Let me know if you need anything," Livvie said. "You okay to walk to your room?"

"Absolutely," I said. "I'm great, really."

I smiled and left her office. My stride slowed as I approached my dorm room. Okay, okay. I still felt a little wobbly. But I was being ridiculous—I needed to pull it together. I put my hand on the doorknob and before I could even turn it halfway, the door flew open and Paige stood there, staring at me.

"Omigod, Sasha!" She hugged me carefully and took my arm to lead me over to sit on my desk chair. "I got a text from Nicole that she heard you fainted. I called you a zillion times and you never answered. Then I called the infirmary and they wouldn't tell me anything—something dumb about patient confidentiality."

"I'm so sorry I didn't call," I said. "My phone's back in the stable. I left everything there and went right to the infirmary. Heather actually walked me to the nurse and she stayed with me until I was released."

Paige sat at her own desk chair and scooted it closer to me. "Heather? Wow. You must have really freaked her out when you fainted. I'm sorry I wasn't there."

I leaned back in my chair, swiveling it a little. "It's not your fault. And she was pretty cool about the whole thing."

"What do you need? Can I make you something to eat or get you anything?" Paige asked.

"No," I said. "Thanks. I got excused from all of my classes tomorrow and I didn't even need it. But whatever—I'll take it."

Paige nodded at my bookcase. "You can actually relax and spend the whole day reading the new books you got over the summer. And you can watch E! all day. You know they'll have marathons of something amazing. I'll be texting you whenever I can to make sure you're okay. And we can have a quiet night tonight. A movie or something and we can go to bed early."

"That sounds perfect," I said. "I love that idea. I'm going to shower and get into cozy pj's. You pick the movie, okay?"

Paige nodded. "Will do."

When I emerged from the shower, I towel-dried my hair and braided it. I just didn't feel up to blow-drying it, and who cared since I wasn't going to class tomorrow.

I got on top of my comforter and covered up with my snuggly blanket.

"I narrowed it down to two comedies," Paige said. She held up the DVD boxes. "Preference?"

I covered a yawn. "Either one is great."

"I'll surprise you, then," Paige said. She put in the DVD and before she could press play, someone knocked on our door.

Paige opened it and Nicole, one of my friends from the stable, peered inside, looking at me with wide eyes.

"Oh, Sasha," she said. "Are you okay?"

I knew everyone was just asking because they cared, but if one more person asked me if I was fine . . .

"I'm great," I said. "Paige and I are going to watch a movie, Livvie's bringing dinner later, and I'm going to sleep it off."

"Good," Nicole said, her blond curls falling around her face as she nodded. She handed a bag to Paige. "I grabbed your stuff from the stable," she said to me. "Your phone's in there—I know I wouldn't want to be without mine for a night."

"Me either," I said. "Thanks."

"I'm going to go so you can rest," Nicole said. "Text me if you need anything."

"I will," I said. "Bye."

Paige and I waved her out the door. Paige got settled on her own bed and before the previews had even finished, I fell asleep.

19

DISMOUNT. NOW.

WHEN PAIGE'S ALARM CLOCK WENT OFF THE next morning, I started to jump out of bed. But then I remembered that I'd been excused from classes for the day. I dozed on and off as Paige got dressed and ready for class.

Paige picked up her bag and books. "I'll text you later. *Rest* today, please." She stared me down. That was the *You better listen or else* Paige look.

"I will, I will! Don't worry."

Paige left and I did rest. For five minutes—until I was sure she was away from Winchester and on her way to class.

I pulled on my riding clothes and stuck my head into the hallway. It was empty. Everyone was in class. I tiptoed down the hallway, knowing I had to sneak by Livvie's office. I stopped by her doorway and, holding my breath, listened to see what she was doing.

"Of course I'll e-mail that spreadsheet," I heard Livvie say. "Let me check my files."

I heard her metal cabinet door open and knew she wasn't facing the door. I peeked, just to make sure, and Livvie was shuffling through papers, her back to me. I hurried by and pushed open the door out of Winchester. When it closed quietly behind me, I knew I'd made it. I probably had at least a couple of hours before Livvie came to check on me.

I walked on the far edge of campus, away from the main buildings and sidewalks so I wouldn't run into anyone. When I got to the stable, I entered through the side door and checked the whiteboard near Mr. Conner's office. It said he was at a meeting until nine, and while he was gone, Mike was in charge.

Perfect. If I ran into Mike, I could come up with some excuse why I was riding in the morning by myself. He probably didn't know that the nurse had told me to rest today.

I gathered Charm's tack and headed for his stall. I left his tack on top of his trunk and picked up Charm's tack box.

"Hi, boy," I said, entering his stall.

With a mouthful of hay, Charm looked up at me, looking a little surprised to see me at this time of the day. Usually, I was in class.

"I know, I'm supposed to be taking it easy, but I'd go crazy if I had to rest *all* day," I told him. I hugged Charm and then started grooming him in his stall. "I know I need to practice and just thinking about not riding made me nervous."

I knew I was trying to justify it to myself why I was breaking the rules by being here. But it was true—it made me feel better to be at the stable and doing something other than sitting in my room. And if I got caught . . . I'd handle it.

I finished grooming Charm and slipped out of his stall to grab his tack. I led him out the back door to the outdoor arena behind the stable. Mr. Conner wouldn't be able to see if he came to his office early. Mike was always so busy I doubted he'd notice that Charm was gone for a while.

I mounted and settled in Charm's saddle. The morning air was still semi-cool, but it wouldn't be long before it was hot and gross. We'd have to work hard to get through all of the exercises I wanted to and get Charm cooled

and groomed so I could sneak back to Winchester before Mr. Conner got back.

I started Charm at a walk and we made two laps around the smaller arena. I let him into a trot and I sat deep in the saddle. Charm moved easily and I felt him relax with each lap we made. I wobbled a little as we changed directions, but I gripped the saddle tighter with my knees.

Charm asked for more rein and I allowed him to canter. There were no jumps in this arena, so Charm was free to stretch his legs from one end of the arena to the other. I slowed him to a trot, then a walk. Charm wanted to canter, but I was getting tired. I wasn't going to faint—I knew that—but I was tired.

Deal, I told myself. *You've got to practice.*

I kicked my feet out of my stirrups, crossed them, and urged Charm into a trot again. We made several laps around the arena and I focused on not wobbling in the saddle and on keeping Charm at an even pace. My arms started to shake from holding Charm back. He wasn't even feisty today—just normal Charm—and I wasn't strong enough to hold him.

I ignored the pain and started to post. It made my legs burn, but I needed the strength training. Fainting during another lesson was *not* an option.

After a couple more laps, I put my stirrups back down and took Charm through figure eights. His body bent through the turns and he became suppler with each movement. I kept my gaze straight ahead, trying to fight off the slightly dizzy feeling. There was no way I was stopping.

After another twenty minutes or so, I wanted to work on my posture. I was so into our practice, it shocked me when I saw someone standing near the fence.

Mr. Conner.

Uh.

Oh.

His arms were folded across his chest and his boots thumped into the arena dirt as he stomped over.

"Dismount. *Now*," he said. His eyes were dark and his face reddened.

I dismounted and looked up at him from under the brim of my helmet. "Mr. Conner, I can explain," I said. "Really, I—"

"Give Charm to Mike and come straight to my office," Mr. Conner said. His tone was scary low. He turned and went into the stable.

My fingers shook as I loosened Charm's girth and took him inside. I found Mike filling a water bucket for one of the stable horses.

"Sasha," Mike said. There was obvious surprise in his voice at seeing me. "What are you doing with Charm tacked up?"

I ducked my head. "I just wanted to practice a little. But Mr. Conner caught me and told me to give Charm to you."

I waited while Mike finished refilling the bucket and latched the stall door. He took Charm's reins from me and gave me *the* look. "You could have gotten hurt—and so could Charm."

I nodded, but didn't really agree with him. I was fine and everyone was treating me like I was a little kid. "I *know*."

Mike led Charm away to cool him down and I dragged my feet down the aisle to Mr. Conner's office. He wouldn't ban me from riding, would he? I hadn't even thought about that. Then he'd have to tell Mr. Nicholson in the progress reports. Maybe Mr. Nicholson would decide that I wasn't the right person for the team if I didn't listen to my instructor.

I gulped and forced myself to knock on Mr. Conner's door.

"Come in," he said.

I walked inside and he motioned for me to take a chair

in front of his desk. No matter how many times I'd been in his office, I couldn't help but stare at the ribbons and trophies that lined the shelves behind his desk.

"Sasha," Mr. Conner said, his face still red. "I don't even know where to start. I'm appalled at your actions today. You disregarded specific instructions from the nurse not to ride. Do you have any idea what might have happened if you'd gotten hurt?"

His voice rose with every word and I sank deeper into my chair. My face burned and I swallowed.

"You not only risked yourself and your horse, but you put *my* job on the line," Mr. Conner said. "I will not tolerate that in my stable. It's behavior I did not expect from you, Sasha."

I could barely look at him. "I'm so sorry," I said. "I felt fine and—"

"I don't care *how* you felt," Mr. Conner interrupted, his voice seeming to reverberate off the office walls. "You were told not to ride and you did."

"I'm sorry," I said again, my voice a whisper.

Mr. Conner stared at me for several seconds, making me squirm. "I cannot have a rider in my stable that's not trustworthy."

"Please," I said. "Don't ban me from riding. That's

why I felt like I *had* to come. You're taping the lesson for Mr. Nicholson soon and I don't feel ready."

"And riding while you're supposed to be recovering is helpful?" Mr. Conner questioned. His voice hadn't lost the sharpness.

I stared down at my lap.

"Go back to your room," Mr. Conner said. "I will be speaking with Livvie immediately. I'm not going to ban you from riding, but if you *ever* do something like this again—it won't just be a ban. You'll be off the team permanently. We'll talk about mucking duty when you're feeling better. Please go."

I stood and left his office, trying not to cry. I walked a few steps, closed my eyes and rubbed them. Everyone needed to give me a break. People fainted—it happened—and they needed to calm down. The worried phone call from Mom and Dad yesterday hadn't helped either. They'd wanted to visit to make sure I was really okay, but I'd managed to talk them out of it.

"Sasha?" A familiar voice made goose bumps rise along my arms.

20

NOT YOUR JOB

ERIC STOOD IN FRONT OF ME, HIS HANDS IN the pockets of his jeans and his dark brown eyes locked on my face.

"I heard you fainted yesterday," he said. "Are you okay?"

"How'd you know I was here? And why aren't you in class?"

"I saw you sneaking to the stable, and when study hall started, I ditched for a few minutes."

I forced myself not to take a step back. I hadn't been this close to Eric since Friday. But there wasn't a trace of hostility in his voice. He looked worried—like he still cared. Even after everything.

I managed to nod. "I'm fine. Thanks. I was just exhausted and dehydrated. But I'm okay now."

"You sure?" he asked. "You could have been really hurt."

"I know," I said. "But I wasn't. It happened once—no big deal. I should get back to Winchester."

Eric stepped to the side so I could walk around him. "Sash?" he called after me. "What happened *was* a big deal. Be careful."

I paused, mid-step. That was what I missed most about Eric and had tried to forget. He'd always been so caring and there for me when I'd been going through the Jacob-and-Callie mess. I forced myself to start walking again.

I looked back over my shoulder as I walked. "You're not my boyfriend anymore," I said softly. "It's not your job to worry about me."

I didn't let myself think about Eric for the entire walk back. I stopped by Livvie's office, prepared to explain everything, but she wasn't in. She'd be knocking on my door the second she'd heard what I'd done. I showered, changed my clothes, and grabbed a book that was overdue for a read—*My Friend Flicka*. I settled back on my bed and covered up with a light blanket.

I tried to stop my brain from going, but all it would focus on was Eric and how he'd cut class to see me. I'd hurt him so much, but he'd risked detention to make sure

I was okay. The only way I wasn't falling apart about losing him was because I knew I'd done what I had to do. And if I moped about Eric, people would know I hadn't really been into Jacob like I'd pretended.

I still didn't even know how I felt about Jacob. Everything was so confusing! Eric and I had been perfect together, but Jacob had made me question things.

I opened my book and forced myself to read the words. I don't know how many pages I made it through before I fell asleep.

21

FAINTING SASHA

AFTER I WOKE UP, I REALLY DID FEEL BETTER.
I did homework, read, and then started to get bored. I
glanced at the clock and realized film class started in half
an hour. And really it wasn't a *class*-class—we did more
theater games than work. I was so over people telling me
to rest.

Livvie had showed up when I was reading and hadn't
been happy—at all—that I'd gone riding. I'd apologized,
pretending to agree with her that it had been dumb and I'd
needed to rest. But she was wrong just like everyone else.

I sat up and started getting ready. Livvie hadn't said
I had to stay in my room, so maybe she'd think I'd gone
to the caf or something if she came to my room. And if
Ms. Scott didn't want me in class, she'd make me leave.

I felt good and the fewer classes I missed, the better. At Canterwood, it took longer to complete makeup work than it did to go to the actual class.

I started to text Paige that I was going to theater class and would see her later, but I canceled the text. She'd be furious if I went to class after I was supposed to stay in my room. I left Winchester and walked to the theater building. I wiped drops of sweat from my forehead and wished I'd worn a tank top instead of a T-shirt.

I was halfway to the auditorium when Jasmine walked down the sidewalk toward me. If I hadn't been so tired, I would have run just to get away from her.

"Wow," Jasmine said. "You're actually up and walking. I mean, aren't you supposed to be lying down with a cold washcloth over your head with people coming by every hour to make sure you're still breathing?"

"Whatever," I said. "I'm fine and I'm going to theater."

Jas smiled. "Great strategy. Show up so they all see your pathetic face and they'll feel even sorrier for Fainting Sasha. Everyone's already talking about you. Really was a brilliant move."

"Fainting?" I laughed. "You've got to be kidding me."

"Oh, please," Jas said, focusing her eyes on me. "You wanted Mr. Conner to feel sorry for you before we taped

the lesson for Mr. Nicholson. You'd have the excuse of being 'sick' and who's gonna kick off the new girl if she fainted? I mean, really, I wish I'd thought of it first."

I shook my head. "You're ridiculous. How can someone *faint* on purpose? I could have hurt Charm. If *you* want to try to faint for 'attention,' go for it."

I walked down the aisle and away from Jasmine. She had no idea what she was talking about and I didn't need to waste time on her. There were a zillion other things to worry about.

I got to the auditorium and walked down to the rows of seating in front of the stage. I took my usual seat behind Heather. Jacob wasn't here yet, thankfully.

Heather half-turned her head and when she saw me, she frowned. "What are you doing here? Weren't you banned from classes today?"

"Yeah, but it's theater. We're not going to be taking tests or anything. And I just needed to sleep it off—really. I did that and I'm *fine*."

Heather shrugged. "You keep saying that word whenever you're not 'fine.' You really are the biggest dork I know. You had the option of staying in your room all day doing whatever, but you *chose* to come to class. You're *so* weird."

"Whatever. God, I'm so sick of everyone judging me. Even Mr. Conner. No one gets it."

"Mr. Conner?"

I wanted to slap my hand over my mouth. But then I really thought about it—Heather would probably respect the fact that I'd ridden when I wasn't supposed to. She understood hard-core practicing.

"I went to ride this morning, just for a couple of hours, and Mr. Conner caught me."

Now I had Heather's full attention. She turned completely around in her seat and stared at me. "You did not."

"I did. He called me into his office, told me I shouldn't have been riding and that I really needed to slow down. It was weird—usually he's all about practicing hard. But this time he wasn't. He was furious."

Heather gave me a look like I was the dumbest person she'd ever seen. "Because you *fainted*. I always knew something was wrong with you—but I never thought you'd be so lame that you'd ride when you knew you shouldn't."

I shook my head. "But I had to. I can't miss a day of practice right now. You get that. Don't act like you don't."

"But you love Charm," Heather said. "I guess that's why I'm so surprised. You could have fainted again and he could have been hurt or something."

"I knew I wasn't going to faint," I snapped. "Don't make it sound like I risked my horse on purpose. If I'd even thought I'd faint today, I wouldn't have ridden."

"Okay, okay," Heather said, raising both hands. "But one day off from riding wouldn't kill you."

"Easy for you to say. You and Jasmine have been riding at the best stables since you started. You've had the expensive trainers and you've competed at the top circuits. I haven't." I paused for a second. "You could take *weeks* off from riding and you'd be fine. But I'm not there yet. I've got to practice as much as I can for that tape. It makes me nervous to miss even one day."

Before Heather could reply, Jacob walked past me. He walked over and sat a couple of seats away from me. Heather looked at me for a second, then turned back to face the stage. I caught Jacob looking at me, almost as if he wanted to ask why I was in class, but he didn't. Like Eric, he had no responsibility for me.

Ms. Scott walked to the front of the stage and shuffled through a stack of papers in her hand. I looked down at my lap and took a breath.

"Everyone, turn to page forty-five in your textbook and we'll take turns reading aloud the chapter," Ms. Scott said.

We all got out our books. Ms. Scott called on a guy in the front row and he began reading about the Globe Theater. He read a few paragraphs before Ms. Scott stopped him.

"What interested you about what you read?" Ms. Scott asked him.

"I've heard of the theater, but I didn't know it burned down," the guy said.

Ms. Scott nodded. "It's sad that the theater was rebuilt only to be shut down by Puritans years later."

"It's like book banning," a girl in the front row said. "It makes me so mad."

We spent the rest of the period talking about censorship and how it was still present today like it was during Shakespeare's time. I loved the discussion and Ms. Scott never stopped any of us from saying what we felt. Her class was like Mr. Ramirez's had been last year—I wished it was longer.

After class, I gathered my bag and got ready to leave. Jacob and I hadn't looked at each other once and Heather hadn't said a word to me. I'd focused on class.

I left the theater and walked up the stairs. I passed the ticket counter, but Heather eventually caught up with me and fell into step beside me.

"You really should consider seeing a shrink or going on some kind of medication," Heather said.

"Excuse me?" I asked.

"You're *ridiculous*. Stop going on and on about how you're not a 'real' rider, or whatever, like Jasmine and me. Yeah, we have more experience—get over it. And without a doubt, *I'm* definitely better than you. But you're not a complete loser rider or you wouldn't have made the YENT."

I just stared at Heather, not knowing what to say.

"You and Charm are a great team," Heather said. "So stop talking so much trash about yourself." She grinned. "You've got enough people, like me, who are more than happy to do that for you."

I couldn't help but smile. We sighed simultaneously and walked away from each other.

22

MINT MASKS AND
CITY GIRLS

WHEN I GOT BACK TO MY ROOM, PAIGE WAS
sitting on her bed cross-legged, reading a magazine. She
looked at me and frowned.

"Where were you?" she asked. "I thought you were
going to stay in all day."

"I just went to theater class," I said. "It was an easy
class and I was feeling good before it started."

"But you were supposed to take the entire day off," Paige
said. "Did Ms. Scott say anything to you about being there?"

"Nope. She either didn't know I wasn't supposed to
be there or she just let me stay. She would have made me
leave if she thought I was sick or something."

Paige shrugged. "I guess. I just hope you got enough
rest to get back to classes and everything tomorrow."

"I'm okay," I said. "Really. I feel great and totally ready for tomorrow."

I knew better than to tell Paige about riding this morning. I didn't think she'd hear about it from anyone, but if she did—I'd tell her then. I didn't want to unless I had to—she'd freak if she found out.

"So, it's Friday night," I said. "We *have* to do something. Any ideas?"

Paige looked up at the ceiling for a second. "I think we should stay in for sure. Want to finish half of our homework so there's not so much? I picked up all of your assignments."

"Yeah, let's definitely do that," I said. "Then we won't have to worry about getting all of it done at once."

Paige nodded. "Perfect."

"How about a homework incentive?" I asked. "If we stay focused and get half of our homework done, let's give ourselves manis, pedis, and facials tonight."

Even though I'd done my nails a couple of nights ago with the Trio, the polish had already chipped from being in the stable.

"Love it," Paige said. "I'm starting *right* now."

We smiled at each other and Paige picked up a few pages from her desk. "These are your assignments," she said.

"Thanks."

I took them from her and went to my desk. We both wanted to get finished, so we had to sit away from each other or we'd start talking and gossiping.

I opened my math book and started the problems Utz had assigned. It didn't take long for me to get through all twenty-five. The new graphing calculator Dad had insisted that I get before school started—even though it was, like, the size of a laptop—made things so much faster.

There was only one chapter to read for history class and I took notes while I read. I turned in my chair, peeking over at Paige, who was leaning over her desk, scribbling furiously.

An hour later, I closed my notebook for Mr. Davidson's English class. I spun my chair and looked at Paige. "Half done!"

"We're in crazy synch," Paige said. "'Cause I'm finishing the last answer for my science class and then I can quit too."

While Paige finished, I gathered my books and papers and shoved my notebooks into my book bag.

"And . . . done too!" Paige said.

I high-fived Paige. "Rocked the homework," I said.

"And now we get to have fun. I think we should do

those mint facials that we got last week and while they dry, we do our nails."

"Yes! Let's go all out—hot washcloths to open our pores, a scrub, and then we apply the mask."

"Love. Done."

Paige and I put on our cozy terry cloth robes and pulled our hair into ponytails.

"Let's wrap our hair up with towels, just like at a real spa, so we won't get face mask in our hair," I suggested.

Paige grabbed two towels and we swept up our hair. We ran water until it was as hot as we could get it, filled the sink, saturated the washcloths, and wrung them out.

I put mine on my face and sighed happily as the heat warmed my face. After a couple of minutes, my cloth started to cool. I pulled it off and Paige did the same. We looked in the mirror at the same time. Our faces were Bazooka bubble-gum pink.

"That felt *so* good," Paige said. "Now for the scrub."

We passed the tube of apricot scrub between us and started rubbing it into our faces in small circles. I felt skin slough off, and the sweet scent of apricot was as relaxing as the steaming hot towel had been.

"Rinse time," I said. We took turns washing the scrub off our faces.

"My face feels *so* soft," Paige said. She ran her finger over her cheekbone. "And now we apply the masks."

Paige picked up a tube of a minty face mask and squeezed some into my palm. I dabbed my fingers into the creamy mixture and spread it over my cheeks, forehead, chin, and nose.

I looked over at Paige and she'd painted giant green circles on her cheeks like a clown. I grinned.

"Don't smirk at me," Paige said. "You're the one who looks like she's ready for Halloween."

"Only my fave holiday," I said. "I mean, I love Christmas, but Halloween's the best."

Paige nodded. "I love it too. But Fourth of July's my favorite. Fireworks. Hot dogs. Cotton candy."

I made a face, causing my now-drying mask to crinkle. "*Your* mom let you get hot dogs and cotton candy? Wouldn't she take you to some Manhattan party for fancy food?"

Paige rolled her eyes. "She does. *Every* year. But my cousin visits from DC and she sneaks out of the party with me and we get all of the real Fourth of July food from street carts. It's amazing. One year, I'm going to find a way to convince my parents to let me go to Coney Island to see the Fourth of July hot dog eating contest. It's supposed to be *insane*."

I smiled. "We could have our own contest when I stay with you during fall break," I said. "And we can eat tons of food from different vendors."

Paige nodded. "We'll get *every* kind of food—I know the best cart that serves Indian food that you'll love."

"I've never had Indian food before. I can't wait."

And I couldn't. Maybe break with Paige wouldn't be so bad. She hadn't asked one question about what had happened over the weekend. She finally got that I didn't want to talk about it, and things were starting to feel like our old friendship.

"You know who else lives in New York," I said, raising an eyebrow. "Someone we'll definitely *not* run into if we sneak off to Coney Island."

"Who?" Paige asked.

"Heather. I don't remember what part of the city she lives in, but I'm sure it's somewhere fancy."

"NYC is so huge that we have *zero* chance of running into her," Paige said. "So don't even worry."

We grabbed our container of nail polishes and sat in the middle of the room. Our collection had grown considerably over the summer. We each brought at least half a dozen new bottles of new polish with us.

"Okay, you pick for me and I'll choose yours," I said.

"Deal." Paige leaned over and peered at the choices. She picked up a couple of different bottles before finally handing one to me. "This is it."

"I love it," I said. It was a pretty copper that had a hint of metallic—perfect for fall.

"And for you . . ." I looked at the two choices I'd narrowed it down to. "Shimmery purple."

"Oooh, fun," Paige said.

"It pops with your skin tone," I said. "It'll look great."

We painted our nails, waited for them to dry and then inspected each other's nails.

"Gorge," I said. "Purple was so the perfect choice."

"The copper goes really well with your tan," Paige said. "Plus, it's very in for fall."

We washed our faces and got onto our beds. "Sooo . . ." Paige said slowly. "I'm thinking that we could watch a marathon session of *City Girls*."

I mock-rolled my eyes. "You had to 'think' about it, huh?"

Paige laughed and got up to put in the DVD. And for the rest of the night, we gossiped, giggled, and ate junk food. Paige really was my best friend—she'd known exactly the kind of night I'd needed to have.

23

PHOTO OP

ON SATURDAY MORNING, PAIGE AND I LEFT Winchester together. We'd woken up early because we both had a zillion things to do.

"Have a good ride," she said.

"Thanks, and have fun with Geena," I said. "Whatever you decide to make, I hope it's something that involves chocolate."

Paige grinned. "That could be arranged."

We split up and I hurried to the stable. Charm and I needed a solid workout. There were only days before the tape, and we had to practice hard. Like, crazy hard.

I grabbed Charm's tack and took it to his stall.

"Hi, boy," I said, smiling at him as I unlatched the stall door.

Charm pricked his ears and walked up to me. I hugged his neck and clipped a lead line to his halter.

"Let's get you sparkling and then we'll work," I said.

I reached into Charm's tack box and pulled out a hoof pick. I cradled his right hoof in my hand and picked out the muck and dirt. After all four hooves were done, I brushed him and tacked him up.

Hoofbeats clattered down the aisle and I saw Julia and Alison lead Trix and Sunstruck toward me. I unclipped the crossties so they could pass through the aisle.

"Hey," I said. "What're you guys doing?"

"We're taking them for a jog on the trails," Alison said. "Sunstruck needed to get out of his stall and I actually thought he'd rather spend time with me than be ridden by Mike."

"I'm sure," I said. "Mike's not you or Julia, so I'm sure Trix and Sunstruck are glad just to be with you guys no matter what you're doing."

Julia patted her bay mare's neck. "She hasn't lost any of her muscle tone, thanks to Mike. And I know us hand walking them isn't enough, but we just wanted to hang out with them today."

I waved my hand. "You don't have to explain wanting to chill with your horse to me. I get it."

Alison smiled. "Yeah, you and Charm definitely have a bond."

The girls waved and walked away. For a second, I wondered if they'd ride once they got far enough away from the stable, but I knew they wouldn't. That would be it for them if they got caught riding *and* without helmets.

I was just glad—even though the situation was awful—that they were able to spend time with their horses.

I put on my helmet and led Charm to the indoor arena. I started to stick my foot in the stirrup, but the camera caught my eye. Hmmm . . . I could tape a lesson to see how I looked. Then, I'd be able to see for myself what I needed to work on. For a second, I wondered if Mr. Conner would care that I was using the camera, but then I decided he wouldn't mind since I wasn't taking it out of the arena.

I led Charm over to the camera and found the button to turn it on. I mounted and started warming up. Charm was ready to go today—he walked briskly for a few strides before tossing his head and begging for more rein. I couldn't help but smile at his energy. Charm was trotting over ground poles when Jasmine and Phoenix entered the arena. Jas halted the gray, yanking on the reins and halting him by the entrance. She mounted and started him toward us.

No matter what she said—I wasn't going to let her intimidate me out of the arena. I was staying.

"Awww, look," Jas said. "It's Fainting Sasha. Should I stay close in case you start to see spots and fall off?"

"You wouldn't be able to keep up to stay with us," I said. I turned away from her and let Charm into a canter to stretch his legs. His gait was smooth and I didn't bounce in the saddle at all. We made two laps around the arena, passing Jasmine who was still warming up Phoenix at a trot by taking him through figure eights.

I slowed Charm to a walk and thought about areas where we most needed improvement—definitely dressage—and using the camera to critique my moves was the perfect use for it.

I urged Charm to collect his trot. He raised his head and neck, which put more pressure on his hindquarters. His strides became shorter, just like I wanted, and I could feel him pushing more with his back legs.

After a few laps around the area, I slowed him and patted his neck. "Nice," I said. "Now we're going to switch to an extended trot in a sec."

I wanted to give Charm a break and transition him from collection to extension, so I trotted him without being collected for a few laps, then asked him to extend his trot. This time, Charm dropped his head and neck. He extended his stride and I smiled, but stayed focused. He was doing great even though dressage was our toughest area. But Charm felt smooth as we moved around the arena. I caught Jasmine looking at us once or twice as we practiced.

She was working with Phoenix on circles and transitions. I loved how even the gray moved, and he seemed to know what Jasmine wanted before she even asked him. They were an amazing pair—if only she realized what a great horse she had. If she did, they'd be unstoppable.

Jas and I practiced for an hour before I felt I'd put Charm through enough dressage work. I let him walk in lazy circles for a few minutes, then halted him. I did a few stretches in the saddle and when I sat up from touching my right boot toe, Jasmine was stopped next to me.

"What?" I asked.

"That's all you're going to do?" Jas said, shaking her head. "Stretches? I guess Mr. Conner's announcement that our first show was a schooling show made you feel pretty confident that you'd do well."

"It *is* a schooling show. And why do you think stretches mean I'm confident? That makes no sense."

Jas laughed. "Maybe you're not confident—I was

wrong. I meant to say that you're finally realizing you have no chance of staying on the YENT and you're just resigned to doing the 'best' you can, which isn't even close to enough."

"You don't know anything. I'm staying on the YENT and I'm going to impress Mr. Conner and Mr. Nicholson at the show."

Jas dropped the reins and folded her arms, smirking. "You're not as stupid as I thought you were. So you get that it was a test—the whole 'schooling show' thing. No one else is going to practice crazy hard and they're all going to look pathetic next to me. You can practice as much as you want, but it won't help."

"Jas, seriously. *What* is your deal? Why don't you just go back to Wellington already?" I asked. "Doesn't this ever get old for you?"

Charm tensed beneath me, sensing the anger in my voice.

Jas edged Phoenix closer. "You really should be nicer to me. Grateful, actually."

I rolled my eyes. "Grateful? Please. For what?"

"You just should be." Jas's eyes were on mine.

"Whatever. Like I believe anything you say. I've got no reason to be grateful to you for anything."

 **182**

Jas smiled, but it wasn't a happy smile. It was scary and the look on her face almost made me walk Charm right out of the arena.

"Fine," Jas said. "Believe whatever you want. But I helped you more than you'll ever know."

"Then if it's so amazing, tell me. You'd never keep it to yourself, so spill. Unless this entire thing is a bluff."

Jas lifted her chin. "Julia and Alison would *wish* what I'd been hinting at was a bluff."

I kept my eyes on Jasmine.

"They didn't cheat." Jasmine didn't even lower her voice. "I stole papers from them and studied their handwriting. I made the cheat sheets and planted them while they were too busy gossiping about whatever boy drama was going down in Blackwell."

My brain raced as I tried to figure out how to keep her talking, without being too obvious.

"So you did that to them," I said. "You caused Julia and Alison to lose their dreams—their shot at the YENT. And you seem so proud of it."

"I am," Jas said, smiling. "They didn't deserve the YENT. Heather was lucky I didn't have a chance to do the same to her, but I'll still get her."

There wasn't a hint of doubt in Jasmine's voice or on

her face. She believed she ruled the school and could do whatever she wanted.

"You wish," I said. "Heather's so much smarter than *you*. Even if I don't tell her, she'll figure it out and come after you."

Jasmine laughed. "Oh, Sasha. You're still *so* Union. It's just your word against mine. And who's going to believe the girl who's so overtired she blacks out on her horse?"

Jasmine dismounted, loosened Phoenix's girth and led him out of the arena.

I sat in Charm's saddle, trying to figure out exactly what to do. Breathing would be a good first step. I sucked in air—still shocked at what had just happened.

I looked over at the camera, something I'd been trying hard not to do ever since Jas began her arrogant confessional. The red light was still on.

24

UNWANTED
THOUGHTS

AFTER TEN MINUTES OF LEADING CHARM IN circles to cool him out, I walked over to the camera. I stared at it, then turned it off. I started to reach for the button to pop out the mini-DVD, but something stopped me. This was up to Julia and Alison now.

I turned off the camera and led Charm to his stall. Inside my wooden tack trunk, I found my phone.

If u want 2 get back on team, take DVD from arena camera. Now.

I sent the text to both Julia and Alison.

I'd just given them everything they needed to clear their names.

Dazed, I brushed Charm, mucked his stall, and gave him hay. My head was swirling from what I'd just heard. I couldn't even begin to think about what was going to happen to Jasmine. She was off the YENT for sure.

"See you tomorrow, boy," I said, kissing Charm's muzzle.

I left him in his stall and started toward Winchester. When I reached the courtyard, I stopped and sat on one of the stone benches. The place was deserted. Everyone was probably heading to dinner or holed up in their rooms doing homework. I listened to the water trickle from the fountain and couldn't stop the flood of thoughts about everything that had happened this week.

Eric and I were broken up. We'd never get back together.

Jacob liked me, but was staying with Callie because he'd promised he would, to spare her feelings at my request.

Paige and I were getting our BFF vibe back, but it was still kind of weird.

The Trio and I had a sort-of-alliance.

And I'd lost my other BFF, Callie, forever.

I looked up from my lap and saw an image of Jacob standing in the spot he'd been in when he'd asked me to give him another chance. That moment last spring felt as if it was replaying right now in front of me. His green eyes had never been so intense and there was emotion behind every word. He'd been sorry about how he knew it would hurt Callie's feelings if he left her for me, but he couldn't stop himself from telling me how he felt.

I can't stop thinking about you.

That's what he'd said. And I couldn't get it out of my brain. I wanted to. I knew I needed to be on my own and I wanted Callie and Jacob to stay together. But every time I thought about Jacob . . .

But then I saw Callie's face at my birthday party when I'd told her I'd been wanting Jacob back for a long time and had tried to kiss him. I'd never seen someone look so betrayed. The look on Callie's face had made me want to sink onto the floor of the Winchester common room and never get up. I thought about the pain on her face every day since it had happened and couldn't stop the twisting of my chest whenever I thought about that night.

I started to get up and leave, but instead I leaned back against the bench. It had been such a crazy week that I needed a few more minutes just to breathe. Every time I thought about my party, it almost made me freeze. I couldn't process what felt like thousands of images that flashed in front of me from that night. It had been one of the worst days of my life. But I'd done what I had to do and I wouldn't change anything I'd done that night. Things were awful now, but I was still here. Still on the YENT. Still doing well in my classes. I had to stop thinking that there was any way I'd repair any of the relationships I'd destroyed. They were over. I had to keep going.

25

ELEVATOR TO AWKWARD, PARTY OF THREE

I FINALLY LEFT MY SPOT ON THE BENCH and headed back to Winchester. While I walked, I decided not to tell Paige about the tape. Julia and Alison hadn't texted me and I wanted to wait until I was sure—either way—before I told Paige what had happened with Jasmine.

When I opened the door to my room, Paige was sprawled on her bed watching a movie.

"Hey," I said. I kicked off my riding boots and peeled off my socks.

Paige paused the film. "How was your ride?"

"Awesome," I said. "Charm and I had a really great workout."

Paige smiled. "Good. Want to get cleaned up and finish *High School Confessions* with me?"

"Absolutely. Be out in five."

I grabbed jeans and a blue T-shirt with capped sleeves.

By the time I showered and towel-dried my hair, Paige had produced two sodas and a bowl of buttery popcorn.

"Thanks," I said, accepting the can of Diet Coke that Paige handed me.

We settled on her bed, the bowl between us, and watched the movie we'd seen a hundred times and could quote lines from. It was one we watched whenever we couldn't decide what to pick or if there was nothing on TV.

When the credits rolled, we looked at each other and laughed. "When she trips down the stairs and drops her tray," Paige said. "I know I'm not *supposed* to laugh, but I can't help it. It's too funny."

"What does that say about us if we laugh at things like that?" I asked, grinning.

Paige got up and stretched. "That we're kind of mean, but we own it."

"Ex-actly."

We laughed and I loved how things felt right at that moment. It was what I'd needed—time by myself to think and then zero weirdness from Paige.

Paige looked over at her desk, then back at me. "Ugh,"

she said. "The rest of our homework. And I have to study for a history quiz."

I looked over at my own desk. "I've got a lot to do too. And I'll probably have to even study tomorrow."

Paige nodded. "Same."

"Let's go to the library and get it done there," I said. "I saw Jasmine at the stable and if I run into her now in our common room, it would be *way* too soon."

"Gotcha. And there are too many distractions in here. Let's go."

I slid my feet into black flip-flops and grabbed my book bag. When I put it over my shoulder, I almost tipped to the side. I was kind of surprised that the handles hadn't torn off yet from the crazy weight of everything I was carrying.

Paige got her bag ready and we left.

"I was thinking," Paige said. "What if we go out to dinner after we study? Now that we can order food—we could get something fun and maybe eat at the media center?"

"Sounds good to me," I said. "We'll have to get something we haven't had in forever—like Chinese or Mexican."

"Perfect," Paige said. She looked at me for a second, then at the sidewalk.

"What's wrong?"

Paige shook her head. "Nothing's wrong. I just feel bad about asking you this and you can say no, but would you mind if I invited Ryan?"

"Paige! Of course I don't care. Text him the second we get to the library and see if he wants to meet us. It'll be fun."

Paige smiled. "I think so too. I just didn't want to make you feel weird or anything."

"It's *not* weird," I said. "I want him to hang out with us. Unless you guys want to have dinner alone?"

"No way," Paige said quickly. "I want you there and if Ryan can come, then it's a bonus."

We reached the library and started up the thousand stone stairs that led up to the entrance. Okay, okay. It was more like twenty—Paige and I had counted one day when we were bored—but my heavy bag made it feel like way more. We walked through the glass-and-gold revolving doors and stopped in the lobby.

We looked at the stairs, then at the elevator. "Laziness all the way," I said.

"Done," Paige said. She pushed the button and we waited for the elevator doors to open. Out of habit, I pulled out my phone to check if I had any texts. Not that

I would—Paige was my only friend and no one else was texting me right now. The door dinged and without looking up, I stepped into the elevator, following Paige.

The doors closed and I realized there were three of us in the elevator.

Paige.

Callie.

And I.

Paige, standing between Callie and me, looked over at Callie and gave her a friendly smile.

"Hey," Callie said, obviously saying it to Paige. She'd pulled her long black hair back with a skinny white headband that looked amazing.

"You here to study too?" Paige asked.

I kept my eyes on the elevator buttons, willing the elevator to move faster. It shouldn't take so long to get to the seventh floor!

"Yeah," Callie said. Her voice was calm and friendly toward Paige. None of her words were directed to me—it was completely a conversation between them. "My English teacher gave us so many pages to read over the weekend—he should have just assigned the entire book."

Paige laughed. "Been there. But you'll get it done."

I hated every second of this.

My best friend and forever ex-best friend were having a conversation as if I weren't inches away from them. I wasn't mad at Paige—she had every right to talk to Callie. They'd been friends pretty much since I'd met Callie.

Callie and I didn't look at each other once. The elevator door opened and all three of us stepped forward at the same time. I dropped back, letting Paige and Callie out first.

"See you, Paige," Callie said. She smiled at Paige—like she used to smile at me—and walked away.

"I'm sorry," Paige said, turning to me and touching my arm. "I'm still trying how to figure out what my relationship is with Callie. It's—"

"Don't," I said. "Really. You guys are friends and you should be. So don't even apologize for talking to her."

Paige nodded, not saying anything. I started walking—not wanting to continue the conversation. We walked past dozens of dark wooden bookcases until we reached our fave table. Luckily, it was empty.

"We should just hang a 'reserved' sign on this table," Paige said. "And maybe people would think the librarians did it or something."

"I love it. This is *the* only table where we do our best work."

"It's because no one ever comes up here and the librarians aren't stalking us like we're going to eat something or try and smuggle in a drink."

"They have been more stalkery than usual," I said. "They should know that the only reason we come here *is* to work. Why would we be up here on the ancient, musty book floor anyway?"

Paige grinned. "So. True."

We unloaded our book bags and sat down. Paige took out her phone and started texting. After a few seconds, she closed the phone.

"Okay. I texted Ryan. We'll see what he says."

Paige put the phone on the table and had barely moved her hand when the phone buzzed. She grabbed it so fast, she almost knocked it off the table. She flipped it open and the second I saw her smile—I knew.

"He said yes," Paige said. "He said to text him whenever we're done with studying and he'll meet us here and we'll walk over together."

"Awesome," I said. "We can grab a room with a giant flat screen and watch something we'd all like."

Paige wrinkled her nose. "Like . . . what? Football? What do boys watch? I don't want to pick something that's girly that he'd hate."

"He'd feel the same way about watching something for guys," I said. "He'd probably be uncomfortable if he was watching sports and you weren't into it. So we'll channel surf and find something for all of us—something funny and easy to watch. No worries."

"Okay." Paige let out a breath and opened her book.

Then she closed it. "Should I go change my clothes or something?" she asked.

I eyed her black keyhole top, vintage jeans, and red ballet flats. "Nope. You look great," I said.

"Okay," Paige said again, smiling. She reopened her book.

Paige was getting more and more comfortable with Ryan, but she was still awkward around him just like I'd been for months with Jacob. I was glad she trusted my advice and that this was something I could help her with.

We started on the rest of our homework and I tried to shake off our—well, *Paige's*—interaction with Callie. I'd made my choice to lie about what had really happened with Jacob to protect Callie's feelings and I had to stick with it. I'd never tell Callie the truth and that meant she'd never be my friend again. But in a way, I felt like I deserved it. Eric had been the perfect boyfriend and I'd

been confused about my feelings—thinking I liked Jacob. I didn't deserve either guy.

I directed my attention back to my homework. This was what things were going to be like for a long time. But sometimes, all I wanted was for things to go back the way they used to be. Eric and I—so happy and building our relationship. Callie being my best friend and the only person I wanted to talk to the second I got to the stable. I wanted Jacob and I to be . . . friends. Right? Friends. But most of all, I wanted a complete do-over at my birthday party.

Stop thinking about it, I told myself. *It's over. Done. Just keep focusing on riding and school.*

I pushed the thoughts out of my brain and for the next two hours, Paige and I worked. Paige lifted her head and put down her pen.

"We're done, right?" Paige asked. "I mean, we can stay longer if you want, but my brain is overloaded."

"Mine too. It *is* Saturday and look—we're, like, the only ones here. Text Ryan and tell him we're done."

While Paige texted him, I cleared off my side of the table. Paige's phone buzzed and she nodded at it.

"He'll meet us out front in five minutes," Paige said. "Should we gloss first?"

I smiled. "You're asking *me* that question?"

We took our stuff into the bathroom and I pulled out my lip gloss bag. The zipper would barely close on the purple-and-white-striped bag—it was so full. I picked up a new flavor—vanilla cherry—that I'd found a few days ago in my old makeup bag. I carefully applied my gloss and Paige did the same. I handed her my purse brush and after she ran it through her red-gold hair, I brushed my hair and pulled it into a low messy bun—pulling out pieces to make it look less balletlike and more beachy.

"Ready?" I asked.

Paige nodded. "I think so. Let's go."

We left the library and walked down the steps. Ryan was waiting on the sidewalk just like he said he would be. He smiled at us, but his grin got wider when he looked at Paige. He was the perfect guy for Paige—sweet, smart, and cute. But he didn't act like he knew he was hot— that's what made him even better. His short, dark brown hair contrasted with his fair skin and his eyes were an intense bluish-green.

"Good idea about eating out," Ryan said. "My roommate said the caf was serving something gross tonight—meatloaf?"

We shuddered collectively.

"Yep, it was definitely the right choice," I said. "Paige and I were just saying that we were in the mood for something different tonight. Chinese or Mexican?"

Ryan nodded. "Ooh, Chinese sounds awesome—it's been a while since I've had it."

"Me too," Paige said. "I haven't had it since I got back to school and I ate it, like, once a week all summer. My mom always tries to order from this fancy place, but whenever she's not home I order it from a tiny restaurant a few blocks away that serves it the best."

"We'll probably end up getting an order of everything," I said, smiling. "You're making me hungry."

Ryan nodded. "I'm in."

Tonight was going to be fun. Paige and Ryan would be together and I didn't have to do anything but relax.

26

F-LIST CELEBS AND CHINESE FOOD

TOGETHER, WE WALKED INTO THE ALREADY-crowded media center. It was packed, like it was every other Saturday night, and the busyness of the place made me want to escape to one of the quiet rooms. I had a feeling that Eric, Jacob, or Callie could be here, and I didn't want to be standing in the lobby if they walked through.

"I'll go get the Chinese food menu," Ryan said. "Be right back."

Ryan went over to the media center monitor and came back with it, and we headed away from the concessions and theater and toward the TV rooms. At the end of the carpeted hallway, we found an empty room. The sand-colored walls made it feel relaxing and it was one of the smaller rooms with a couch, single recliner, flat screen, and coffee table.

"This okay with you guys?" Paige asked. Her eyes darted from mine to Ryan's. I had a feeling the look she had in her eyes was the same as when I'd met up with Jacob at the media center for the first time.

"It's great," Ryan said.

I nodded. "It's ours now."

We all put down our bags. I sat on the cushy black leather recliner and popped up the footrest. "Ahhh," I said. "This *so* beats the library."

Paige and Ryan laughed. Ryan sat down first at the end of the couch and Paige scooted next to him. I hid my smile—I liked seeing them close together and it made me happy that Paige was getting more and more comfortable with Ryan.

"Totally," Paige said. "It's ridiculous. Sasha and I did homework on Friday, we did more today, and we've still got to study tomorrow."

"You're not alone," Ryan said. "It's crazy for me, too. I thought the teachers expected a lot out of us from seventh grade, but this year has been insane and it's barely started."

"I think we should make a pact not to talk about school anymore tonight," I said. "Deal?"

Paige and Ryan nodded.

"Let's order and watch TV," Ryan said. We all leaned

over the menu and decided what we wanted.

"Want to get a bunch of stuff and share?" Paige asked.

"Definitely," I said. "Let's do it."

We picked cold sesame noodles, spinach dumplings, sesame chicken, and an order of wonton soup. Ryan placed the order and my stomach growled as I listened to him list the different foods.

"It'll take about half an hour," Ryan said. "I'll go pick it up at the counter."

We settled into our seats. Paige picked up the remote and turned on the TV. She flipped through the channels and at the same second we all said, "That!" when the reality TV show that only everyone was talking about came on. The show had F-list celebrities who'd never done anything other than acting work "regular" jobs.

"This is only the most ridiculous, and by ridiculous I mean awesome, show ever," Paige said.

"It's at that embarrassingly awful level," Ryan said.

We laughed as pop star Nala spent the day as a zookeeper. She tried to feed the seals and when one started to move toward her for a fish, she screamed, dropped the fish, and ran. The episode ended and just as a rerun started, Ryan got up.

"Almost forgot about the food," he said.

Paige and I hopped up and grabbed our student cards for Ryan to split the food on all of our cards.

He walked out and Paige turned to me, her eyes bright. I knew what she was feeling—just like I'd felt the first time I'd gone out with Jacob.

"It's going great, right? Or is it just me?"

I smiled. "It's going *perfect*. He's having so much fun and he keeps looking at you."

"He does?" Paige asked, blushing.

"He does. He really likes you—he's obviously enjoying hanging out."

I could relate to Paige's insecurities. I'd felt the same way when Jacob and I had been paired up in film class and had to spend time together. I'd thought about every word out of my mouth and wondered if everything I'd said had sounded dumb.

We both turned to the door when Ryan walked through, carrying our bag of food.

"Thanks," Paige said.

"Sure," Ryan said, smiling. He set the bag on the coffee table and we all moved to the floor to spread the containers on the table. We piled our plates with food and dug in.

"So. Good," I said, my mouth full.

"Mmm hmm," Paige said.

Ryan, Paige, and I ate and watched the repeat episode. Paige, sitting between Ryan and me, kept sneaking glances at Ryan and I wondered if I'd been that obvious when I'd crushed on Jacob—the first guy I'd ever liked. Paige had also never sat that close to Ryan and I watched as they were almostbutnotquite touching.

I ate another bite of my spinach dumpling and when I glanced at Paige and Ryan again, I saw Jacob and me. The way Ryan interacted with Paige was how things had started with Jacob. Easy. Friendly. I tried to concentrate on my food, but I suddenly couldn't swallow. I saw images of Jacob and wondered what would have happened if that awful night at the Sweetheart Soirée had never happened. Then that made me start to think about Eric.

I took a breath and forced myself to sit up straighter. It did no good to think about that now. I couldn't be with either guy, so what was the point of thinking about them? Watching Paige and Ryan together made me happy for them—not jealous. I'd done everything I'd needed to do to protect my friends and I wasn't going to think about Jacob now.

Or ever.

We finished eating and stuffed our trash into the bag.

"I'm so full," Paige said. "That was amazing."

"Me too," Ryan said. He flipped open his phone, checking the time. "I can watch another episode, but then I've got to go for a dorm meeting."

"Cool," Paige said.

The episode flew by and Ryan stood and stretched when it ended.

"I had fun," he said. "I'll text you?"

For a second, I thought Paige wouldn't be able to speak. But instead, she grinned and took a step closer to Ryan. "Sounds good," she said. "See you."

Ryan smiled at both of us, got off the couch, and walked out of the room. For a second, I saw Jacob walking away—not Ryan. I shook it out of my brain.

Paige waited exactly five point two seconds before turning to me and grabbing my arms.

"Ohhhhmmyyygod," Paige said. "That was *awesome!*"

"You were so cool," I said. "He likes you so much. He already wants to text you but doesn't want to look like a dork, I know it."

"Just knowing that you think he wants to text me already is enough," Paige said. Her eyes sparkled and she bounced up and down.

We gathered our stuff, linked arms, and left the media center.

"That was the perfect distraction from tomorrow," Paige said.

"What's tomorrow?" I asked.

We walked down the stairs and to the sidewalk.

"Nominations for Homecoming prince and princess will be posted!"

I made a face.

"C'mon," Paige said. "It'll be fun. Everyone gets into it—it's almost like a break from school because even the teachers realize everyone's so excited about it that they don't expect us to concentrate."

"I'm excited for you, 'cause you'll definitely be nominated," I said. "But I really could skip everything else and be happy."

Paige bumped her shoulder against mine. "You're not going to skip everything, and we'll have fun together—I promise."

I smiled for Paige's benefit, but started thinking of ways to attend as few Homecoming events as possible. I needed a list of excuses ASAP.

27

THE LIST

"OMIGODOMIGOD!" SQUEALS RANG DOWN the hallway and bare feet slapped against the wooden floors as what sounded like a dozen people ran by Paige's and my room *verrry* early the next morning. Like six fifteen early.

I sat up straight in bed, heart pounding, and watched as Paige jumped out of bed, put on her pink robe, and slid her feet into flip-flops.

"What's going on? Is there a fire?!" I asked. I didn't hear an alarm, but maybe they were broken or out of batteries. What would I grab first? I threw back my covers and headed for my lip gloss collection.

Paige laughed. "It's not a fire. Homecoming nominations must have been posted in the common room. C'mon!"

"I thought it was something serious!" I grumbled. "People were running down the hallway for *nominations*?" I flopped back onto my bed and pulled my blanket over my face.

"Sasha!" Paige grabbed me by the wrist and pulled me up. "You're coming. Right now."

"Okay, okay," I said, my whining only half-serious.

Paige shifted from foot to foot as I pulled on my own robe and started looking for shoes. I couldn't find the pair I wanted and I could tell Paige was about to implode if we didn't leave.

"Let's go," I said. "Who cares about shoes this early in the morning."

Paige yanked open the door and hurried into the hallway. I closed it behind us and we followed girls who seemed to be coming from every level of Winchester to the common room.

I let Paige—who was usually the most polite person ever—elbow her way through the crowd of girls and get up to the corkboard. Posted on the side was a pink sheet of paper with a clear tack.

"Omigod! She got nominated!"

"Aww, I didn't."

"Ooooh, but you did!"

The endless chatter about who made it and who didn't filled the common room.

"Sasha," Paige said. She reached back and dragged me forward. A couple of girls glared at me and moved away. I scanned the list and started blinking at what I was seeing. This couldn't be right.

8th-grade girls:

Paige Parker

Heather Fox

Nicole Allen

Callie Harper

Sasha Silver

8th-grade boys:

Eric Rodriguez

Jacob Schwartz

Troy Brown

Ben Wells

Ryan Shore

"Please tell me that my name is *not* on that list," I said to Paige. "Who would do that? I don't even want to go to Homecoming!"

"Wow, talk about ungrateful," I heard someone stage-whisper behind me. I didn't even turn around to try and figure out who it was. I didn't want to see Jasmine's face.

Paige put her hand on my arm and steered me through the crowd and out of the common room.

"Sash, you should be *thrilled* to have your name on that list," Paige said. "It's a huge honor. I know you're upset about whatever happened last weekend, but this will be good for you—trust me. It'll be a distraction from everything going on."

I shook my head. "But I don't need a distraction. I'm busy enough with school and riding. Can I go to Headmistress Drake and ask to have my name taken off?"

Paige shook her head. "No way. You were voted by your peers—she'd never let you do that."

I groaned and walked with Paige back to our room. Now I was forced to go to *every* Homecoming-related event. Ridiculous. I wondered it was some kind of joke and that people just chose my name to force me to be in the spotlight when they had to know I didn't want to be. Maybe they just wanted to see me sweating next to Callie, Jacob, and Eric.

Back in our room, I put on my riding clothes. Then I realized something awful.

"Oh, Paige," I said, turning to her. "I'm such a jerk. I didn't even say congratulations. This is a big deal for you—it's HUGE. Seriously, I'm sorry."

Paige nodded. "It's okay. You were upset—no big deal."

"No, it *is* a big deal. Even if I'm not into it, I'm excited for you. We'll have to get something from the Sweet Shoppe later. My treat."

Paige smiled. "That sounds great."

28

UNWILLING PRINCESS
IN TRAINING

WHEN I REACHED THE STABLE, I WENT straight to Charm's stall and threw my arms around his neck. He sniffed my hair and held still, letting me lean against him. He was my only constant.

"Argh!" I said. "Are you kidding me?" I let go of Charm's neck, leaned against the stall wall, and sank into the sawdust.

"I did not want to be Homecoming *anything*," I continued. Charm lowered his head, taking in my rant and listening to every word. "I know it's just a nomination and there's no way I'll win, but I don't even want to participate at all."

All I wanted to do was focus on school and riding. Homecoming was supposed to be Paige's thing where she'd tell me about it, and just hearing stories from her would be fun. *That* I could've handled. But now I had to be involved in everything and around everyone. Callie. Jacob. Eric.

Last year, I'd been so overwhelmed by being the new girl that I'd missed anything Homecoming-related. So I had no clue how any of it really worked, what I'd be doing, or how much time I'd have to spend with Jacob, Eric, and Callie.

I looked up when a head poked over the stall door.

"Hey," Paige said. "Can I come in?"

"Sure." I got up and helped her unlatch Charm's stall. I had to smile when I watched Paige pat Charm's shoulder and look comfortable around him. I remembered how tentative Paige had been around Charm the first time she'd met him. But now she was a total pro—she knew how to groom and she could walk and trot.

But as I watched Paige closer, I knew something was up. She was tugging at the ends of her hair like she did when she was nervous. Paige sat on the clean sawdust next to me and we both giggled when Charm meandered over to us and stuck his head down to nose Paige's hand with his muzzle.

"He's offended that you came to visit without a treat," I said. "How dare you."

Paige bowed her head. "So sorry, Charm. I'll come back with *two* carrots next time—promise."

That seemed to satisfy Charm. He walked to the other end of his stall, cocked a hind leg, and started to fall asleep.

"I wanted to talk more about Homecoming," Paige said, turning her head to look at me. "I know you don't care about it. And I get it! I really do—you have to be around people that will make you feel uncomfortable. But you can't let them ruin it for you."

Interest level? Still zero.

"The whole thing is just supposed to be fun. Not something to make you anxious."

I nodded. This wasn't about Homecoming. Paige was working up to talk to me about something else—something bigger.

"We can do everything together," Paige continued. "Whatever activities there are—I'll be there, obviously. I won't let Callie, Jacob, or Eric make things weird for you. I *promise*."

"Thanks," I said. "I knew you'd be there for me. But . . . I know you." I eyed Paige. "Why do you *really* look so worried? You didn't come here to talk more about Homecoming."

Paige drew her knees up to her chest and rested her chin

on top. "You're right—this isn't just about Homecoming. I mean, part of it was because I *really* do want you to give Homecoming a chance, then decide if you really hate it. But I've watched you since last weekend, Sasha, and I'm worried."

I shook my head. "I know I scared you when I fainted. And sleeping over with the Trio probably hurt your feelings and I'm sorry if it did."

"It's not that. I want you to do whatever makes you comfortable, and you did. I'm worried about *why* you fainted. You passed out because you were stressed and crazy exhausted. You've been doing this to yourself since the weekend and it's not like you."

I swallowed and looked down. "Paige, I—"

"Just let me finish." Paige's voice was soft. "I expected you to be devastated about Eric *and* Jacob *and* Callie. I thought we'd get through it and eat tons of brownies together and that you'd let me help you. I'm your best friend, Sasha, and you've shut me out this week. If I did something—if there's something going on—I'm asking you to tell me. Trust me like you used to and just talk to me."

I glanced at Paige and saw a mix of hurt and worry on her face. She had always been the first one I'd gone to about everything and she obviously sensed I was hiding

the real truth about what had happened. It made me feel sick that I'd hurt her or caused her to worry about our friendship. That was the last thing I wanted to do.

"Paige, I . . ." my words trailed off. I couldn't even finish my sentence. Paige and I looked at our laps for a couple of minutes, waiting for me to talk, but I fell silent. There was no explanation I could give her. I'd resigned not to tell anyone and I had to stick to it.

"I'm going back to our room," Paige said, getting up and brushing off her jeans. "If you can't talk to me, I guess . . . I guess I'm just wasting my time."

Paige reached over Charm's stall door, feeling for the latch.

"Nothing's changed between us," I said, not wanting to let her walk away. "You're still my best friend."

Paige stared at me for a second. "If that was true, you'd let me help you."

She walked out of the stall and secured the door behind her. I dropped my head into my hands. I had to do something. If I lost Paige, I'd have nothing. Tears burned my eyes. I didn't even know if I wanted to stay at Canterwood if Paige and I weren't friends.

I went back and forth with two options—either telling Paige the truth, which I suspected she already knew,

or come up with a believable lie that she would accept. I hated even thinking the word *lie* since it had gotten me into so much trouble last week. But Paige was way off this time. I was doing what I needed to do with school, riding, and everything else. I couldn't slow down or I'd never stay on the YENT, my grades would slip, and I'd be kicked off the team.

Paige, who hadn't lost any of her friends and was just starting a relationship with Ryan, didn't understand one important thing—that when you lost everything, you had nothing to lose. And if I stopped for one second, I knew I'd realize how much I'd really lost.

29

RIVAL REVENGE

I GOT UP, BRUSHED OFF MY PANTS, AND LED Charm into the crossties. I still wasn't ready to go back to my room and needed something to do. So while Charm was in the aisle, I mucked his stall and gave him a fresh layer of sawdust. I filled his hay net with two flakes of hay, gave him his grain, and decided to clean his water bucket.

I unclipped the bucket from the wall and carried it into the indoor wash stall. I hosed it, soaped it, and filled it with clean water. Then I focused my attention on Charm. I groomed him, taking my time to wash and dry his white sock and his blaze. I grabbed clippers from my tack trunk and trimmed his whiskers and bridle path. I picked his hooves—noting that it would be time for him to be shod soon. I ran a wide-toothed comb through Charm's mane and tail and sprayed them with a leave-in conditioner.

Charm's coat had a soft, coppery sheen when I finished and his blaze and sock were a brilliant white. It made me feel better to see him look and feel his best.

I unclipped him and led him back to his stall.

"Please don't lie down, okay?" I asked. "Just for one day?"

Charm seemed to wink at me—like a tease. I mock-rolled my eyes at him and blew him a kiss. "See you tomorrow, guy."

Charm didn't look up to respond—his face was in his grain bucket as he chewed noisily.

I left the stable and took a different way back to Winchester—a long path that made a loop and went past Orchard. I still needed more time to think about how to handle Paige. I didn't want it to drag on forever—I had to make a decision. And the right one. I scuffed my shoe against the sidewalk and was glad when the sun hid behind the clouds. The air seemed to cool a few degrees almost instantly.

I started past Orchard and saw Heather walking up the stairs. She half-turned and saw me. She started to look back to the door, then focused on me.

"Since you don't have any form of a life, I know you've

got nowhere to be," Heather said. "Come to my room with me for a minute."

"Okay," was all I could get out. I was too surprised to react to her insult.

In silence, we walked to the Trio's suite. Heather opened the door and I followed her inside. Julia and Alison were out and I stood twisting my fingers, unsure what this was about. If Julia and Alison hadn't gotten the DVD, Heather was probably about to inflict a new form of torture that she'd devised just for this occasion.

"Sit," Heather said.

I sat on the couch—the end closest to the door—and Heather walked back and forth from the window to the coffee table before finally sitting on the table's edge.

I'd never needed my soothing mint lip gloss more than I'd needed it now, but it was back in my room. I licked my bottom lip and willed Heather to just say whatever it was.

Heather tucked her blond hair behind her ears. "Julia and Alison got the DVD." She smiled, shaking her head. "They actually got it."

"That's great!" I said. "They're going to be cleared now. Everything just happened at the right moment and

we didn't even have to do anything to Jasmine—she did that to herself."

Heather nodded. "I know. But you . . ." She paused and for a second, I thought I saw tears in her eyes before she blinked a couple of times. "You saved my best friends."

"I hope someone else would have done the same for me. And we never have to talk about it again. I want Julia and Alison to get back on the team and for this entire cheating thing to go away. I have to apologize to them—I thought they really did cheat."

"I understand why you did," Heather said, shrugging. "I wouldn't have believed you either, if the roles were reversed."

"Mutual distrust. I doubt that'll ever go away," I said, half-smiling.

"Never." Heather said it so fast, we both laughed.

"But now that Julia and Alison should be okay, at least you can focus all of that energy on your riding."

"Yeah, if I didn't have that dumb Homecoming nomination."

I had to fight the urge to jump up and hug Heather. "I feel the same way! Everyone's so excited—and that's fine—but I didn't ask to be nominated. I didn't want to participate at all."

"Me either. It's all so lame."

We smiled at each other. Real smiles. Something we actually agreed on. That was kind of happening more often.

"But," Heather continued, "I don't want to be completely consumed by riding again. I've done that my whole life. And I've . . ."

I let a few seconds go by before I asked, "You've what?"

Heather's guard dropped in that moment. I *saw* it happen. Her tough girl attitude evaporated.

"I missed a lot," Heather said, speaking slowly. "My dad was pushing me so hard about riding—and I loved it, really—but there was never a break. I was at a horse show every weekend, training before and after school. My life revolved around winning—not horses or how much I really do love them."

I tried to keep a neutral expression on my face and not show how shocked I was that Heather Fox was admitting these things to *me*.

"So do you regret it?" I asked. "Working so hard and competing like you did?"

Heather shook her head. "Not for a second. Riding professionally is my dream, but it's also got to be something

I love doing. And when my dad's obsessed with it and how many shows I can win, it's not fun anymore. I almost gave up horses—my favorite thing—because of it."

"Did you start riding because you wanted to compete?" I asked.

Heather laughed. "You won't believe this, but I actually pleasure-rode first. I didn't even think about showing until my trainer told my parents I had talent. Then, lessons went from once a week to three times a week and it escalated from there."

"I'm coming from a different place, obviously," I said. "My parents have been supportive of my riding, but they're hands-off. They let me make the decisions about what I do. That's worked great. Until now. They don't see how many hours I'm really in the stable here, or how I'm obsessing over the tape for Mr. Nicholson. So we're both getting pressured—you from your dad, and me from myself."

Heather nodded. She didn't look like she was going to blackmail me with something to be sure I'd never repeat any of this. She needed someone to talk to.

"You're going to become me," Heather said. "If you keep riding like you are, you're going to be obsessed. You won't be able to enjoy anything—movies, TV, whatever—because all you'll be doing is thinking about what riding exercises you could be doing right now, how you messed up that oxer last week, and how many points you need to qualify for championships."

I shifted on the couch. "I'm not obsessed with riding. I just have more time. And I needed to practice more anyway. But I'm not going to have as much time next week with—"

"Homecoming," Heather said, finishing my sentence. "Lucky us—that's going to be *fantastic*." The sarcasm in Heather's voice made me smile.

"Oh, please," I said. "You know you want to win."

Heather laughed. "*You* do. And you know it. But if either of us were to win, you know it would be me."

She smirked at me and I was glad, strangely, to see that side of her back.

"On that note," I said, "I've got to go." I got up and opened the door. "I'll probably win. Maybe that would make the whole thing worth it."

"Oh, God," Heather said. "Delusional, you poor thing."

We both rolled our eyes at each other and I shut the door.

Walking out of Orchard, I felt better than I had in

days. I'd never expected to have a real talk with Heather—especially not one where she opened up about her background with riding. We hated each other most of the time, but it got harder to dislike Heather every moment when we had interactions like that.

Inside Winchester, I walked down the hallway to my room but I stopped for a second, contemplating if I should chance running into Jasmine in the common room and go there for a few more minutes to think more about what I would say to Paige.

I walked a few more steps, passing Jasmine's room. Then I stopped. I backed up and noticed the door was open a few inches. I didn't hear Jas inside, so maybe she'd forgotten to shut the door or something on her way out.

I knocked lightly and waited a few seconds. Silence. I pushed open the door, walked inside, and stopped in the center of her room, trying to process.

It felt like my brain had frozen and I couldn't even understand what I was seeing.

The room was completely bare. Jas's bed was stripped. Her desk, chair, and table were gone. The walls were free of posters and her closet doors were open, revealing nothing but a few empty hangers.

Julia and Alison had gotten their revenge.

ABOUT THE AUTHOR

Twenty-three-year-old Jessica Burkhart is a writer from New York City. Like Sasha, she's crazy about horses, lip gloss, and all things pink and sparkly. Jess was an equestrian and had a horse like Charm before she started writing. To watch Jess's vlogs and read her blog, visit www.jessicaburkhart.com.

Looking for another great book?
Find it
IN THE MIDDLE.

Fun, fantastic books for kids
in the in-beTWEEN age.

IntheMiddleBooks.com

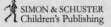

FIVE GIRLS. ONE ACADEMY. AND SOME SERIOUS ATTITUDE.

CANTERWOOD CREST

by Jessica Burkhart

TAKE THE REINS

CHASING BLUE

BEHIND THE BIT

TRIPLE FAULT

BEST ENEMIES

LITTLE WHITE LIES

RIVAL REVENGE

HOME SWEET DRAMA

Don't forget to check out the website for downloadables, quizzes, author vlogs, and more!

www.canterwoodcrest.com

FROM ALADDIN M!X　　PUBLISHED BY SIMON & SCHUSTER